The Legend
of the Lost Gold

"Maybe it's too chilly for a swim," Bess said with a shudder. She wrapped her towel around her shivering body.

"Not for me," George said enthusiastically. "It's perfect." She hurried ahead and eagerly scrambled onto the diving board.

As George raised her arms high over her head, a peculiar sound drew Nancy's attention to the sky. At first she didn't realize what she was seeing. It looked like a long, looping snake flying through the air.

Then, in a chilling moment, Nancy understood. It was the cable from the television satellite tower, and one end was disconnected. The cable was drifting down toward the pool, carrying enough electricity to fry anything in the water.

"George!" Nancy yelled as her friend bounced high in the air off the diving board. "Don't dive!"

Nancy Drew
Mystery Stories

Available from Simon & Schuster

NANCY DREW® 138

THE LEGEND OF
THE LOST GOLD

CAROLYN KEENE

Aladdin Paperbacks
New York   London   Toronto   Sydney   Singapore

First Aladdin Paperbacks edition April 2002
First Minstrel edition August 1997

Copyright © 1997 Simon & Schuster, Inc.
Produced by Mega-Books, Inc.

ALADDIN PAPERBACKS
An imprint of Simon & Schuster
Children's Publishing Division
1230 Avenue of the Americas
New York, NY 10020

Printed in the United States of America

10 9 8 7 6

NANCY DREW and NANCY DREW MYSTERY STORIES are
registered trademarks of Simon & Schuster, Inc.

ISBN 0-671-00049-7

Contents

THE LEGEND OF
THE LOST GOLD

1

Break-in on the Bluffs

"There it is—Opa." Nancy Drew read the sign stretching across the canyon road ahead. "It means good fortune and happiness in Greek."

"Sounds promising," George Fayne said from the backseat. "I could use a little *opa*."

Eighteen-year-old Nancy guided her blue Mustang off the coast highway and through an iron gate. Then she drove up the bumpy winding mountain road to the main building of the Opa tourist lodge in Big Sur, California.

"Wow, this is a perfect place for a week's vacation," Bess Marvin said as Nancy parked the car. "Just look at that view. Hannah was right."

The three got out of the car and looked back down the road. Nancy shielded her blue eyes as she took in the breathtaking view. She said a

1

silent thank-you to her beloved housekeeper back in River Heights, Hannah Gruen, who had suggested this resort for a vacation.

They could see for miles in all directions. Behind them, the tree-covered Santa Lucia Mountains stretched toward the sky. Ahead, the sea glittered white in the late afternoon sun. Around them, the golden hills and dark canyons of Opa led to the rocky cliffs that plunged down to the Pacific Ocean.

"Let's get checked in," Nancy said. Her reddish blond hair glinted in the bright August sun. "The brochure said that Tuesday is barbecue and line dancing night."

"I'm thinking about taking a horseback ride on one of the trails tonight," George said as they hauled their luggage from the trunk of the car.

"Not me," Bess said dreamily, following the others into the lodge. "I'd like to sit on one of those benches and watch the sun set over the ocean—preferably with a nice guy I'll meet at the dance."

George and Bess were Nancy's best friends. Although Bess was George's cousin, people rarely guessed the two were related. Brown-eyed George had close-cropped dark hair and a slim, muscular body, and favored sports and heavy workouts. Bess, who was shorter, with blond hair and blue eyes, jokingly said she loved sports, too, but from the sidelines.

"Hi. I'll bet you're the guests from back east," a pretty young woman said from behind the front

2

desk as Nancy, Bess, and George entered the lodge. "I thought you'd be getting in about now. I'm the owner here—Didi Koulakis. And this is my dear friend and assistant, Betty Myers. Welcome to Opa!"

Didi was pretty in a natural sort of way, Nancy thought. Didi didn't wear much makeup, but really didn't need it. She had deep green eyes and dark hair pulled back with a plastic clip. She was dressed in jeans and a loose embroidered blouse.

Betty Myers was an older woman—she looked to Nancy to be close to seventy—with soft white hair fluffed around her friendly face. "Hannah has told me so much about you in her letters," Mrs. Myers said to Nancy. "I feel as if I know you already. I miss my old friend. How is she?"

"She's wonderful," Nancy said. "She sent you a present—I'll find it when we unpack."

"Let's go right to your cottage and get you settled," Didi said, picking up a suitcase in each hand. Nancy was surprised to see how young the owner was. She seemed to be about Nancy's age.

Didi led the three visitors down a trail through a dense, pungent pine grove to a small cottage perched on a bluff overlooking the ocean. One room served as a living and dining room. It was furnished with antique redwood chairs, a rocker, and a sofa piled high with plump pillows.

A large stone fireplace anchored one end of the room, a small kitchen nook the other. A ladder next to the kitchen led to a sleeping loft overlook-

3

ing the living room. One door across from the fireplace opened to a bedroom, with rustic twin beds and dressers. The other led to a bathroom with an old claw foot tub.

"You two take the bedroom, I'll sleep in the loft," Nancy said to Bess and George, climbing the ladder to take a look. "It's wonderful up here." There was a double bed with a headboard made of bent twigs in a spiderweb pattern. A night table, small bookcase, and dresser rounded out the loft's furniture.

"How soon can you get settled?" Didi asked from below. "I've got time right now to give you a little tour around Opa before I have to check on the kitchen for tonight's barbecue."

"I'm ready now," Nancy said, hurrying back down the ladder. "How about you two?"

"Ready as I'll ever be," George said, dropping her bag in the bedroom. Bess checked her lipstick in the bathroom mirror, then joined the others.

"We have fifty acres," Didi said as the group left the cottage, "and plenty of activities to keep you busy."

They walked past other guest cottages, a swimming pool, and an area cleared for campfire suppers that was surrounded by a tumbling creek. Several riding trails disappeared into deep canyons. Others led down to a bay carved from the ocean bluffs.

Didi stopped at the stables and introduced the man working there. "This is Cal Burns, our stable

4

master and riding guide. He'll help get you matched up with one of our horses and either suggest a trail or take you out on a ride himself."

"Just call me Cal," he said, with a tip of his baseball cap. He appeared to be in his forties, with leathery golden skin and sun-bleached hair.

"Those fellas over there," Cal said, pointing to two young men hoisting a new window into the side of the stable, "are Sam and Barney Shaw. Sam's our new maintenance man and his brother, Barney, is our new stable hand." The two burly men nodded their greeting as they pushed the window into place.

After a quick tour of the stable, Didi led Nancy and her friends back to the main lodge. "I've got to get into the kitchen to see about this barbecue," she said. "Call me if you need anything."

"Thanks," Nancy said. "You've been so gracious. I know we're going to have a great time here."

"I hope so," Didi said with a grin. "See you later."

Didi headed for the kitchen, and Nancy, George, and Bess went back to their cottage to unpack, then shower and dress for the evening's activities. Nancy decided on jeans and a blue, long-sleeved, cropped T-shirt. George chose a red shirt and jeans, and Bess put on a white ruffled blouse and a swirly denim skirt.

Nancy grabbed the present Hannah Gruen had sent along for Mrs. Myers, and the three friends headed for the main lodge.

The building had a dining hall overlooking the ocean, a large party room for dances and receptions, a library, and a game room with card tables, dartboards, and a pool table.

"I didn't realize how hungry I was," George said. "It's been seven hours since we had our lunch at that roadside restaurant. This looks wonderful."

A buffet was set up along one side of the dining room. Barbecued chicken and ribs, potatoes, sliced tomatoes and other raw vegetables, and corn bread were heaped on the main serving table. Side tables offered pies, cakes, and beverages.

"Let's sit outdoors," Nancy said. "You can watch your sunset, Bess," she added with a smile.

"Great," Bess said. "I'll save the moonrise for the guy I'm going to meet at the dance."

Nancy filled her plate, took a glass of pink lemonade, and headed for one of the redwood tables on the long porch outside. Bess and George followed, carrying their plates. They all dug right into the delicious food.

"I see Mrs. Myers," Nancy said, spotting the woman who appeared to be doubling as hostess for the evening. "I'm going to take Hannah's present over."

Nancy wound around the tables until she reached Mrs. Myers, who stood at a small table in the lobby greeting guests. "Oh, it's beautiful, Nancy," Mrs. Myers said as she unwrapped the

6

scarf that Hannah Gruen had sent. "I'll think of Hannah every time I wear it. She's such a dear friend."

Nancy smiled as she thought of Hannah. "Yes, she is," Nancy said. "I don't know what I would have done without her." She thought of how much Hannah meant to her as she'd grown up. Nancy's mother had died when Nancy was three years old, and Hannah had been with Nancy and her father, Carson Drew, ever since.

Mrs. Myers smiled at Nancy and patted her hand. "And now, dear," she said, putting the scarf back in the box, "it's time to return to your friends. I think the dancing's about to start."

Nancy went back to join the others. Didi was herding them to the party room with its large dance floor. A four-piece band struck up a familiar country and western song, and a young couple led the exuberant participants in a lively line dance.

"My feet keep getting mixed up," Bess said, laughing, when the dance was over.

"I don't know—you look pretty good to me," said a young man in jeans and a denim shirt. He looked like a football player, with broad shoulders. He gave Bess a wide smile. "My name's Ken Randell. This is my friend Jay Webb."

Bess introduced herself and her friends. Then they got back in line for the next few numbers. Finally, Nancy, George, and Jay took a break while Bess and Ken paired off for a couples dance.

7

"Looks like Bess is falling in love again," George said while Jay went for sodas.

"How about you?" Nancy teased. "Jay's pretty cute—all that blond hair and those big blue eyes."

Red-faced, George looked around the room. "Well, we'll just have to find someone for you," she said.

"No, thanks," Nancy said with a laugh. "I'll find my own dancing partners, if you don't mind. And besides, I've got my own dancing partner back at home," she added, referring to longtime boyfriend Ned Nickerson.

Jay returned with their sodas. "Are you from California?" he asked.

"No, we're from back east, as Didi says," Nancy answered. "We're staying at Opa on vacation."

"That's great," Jay said. Then he laughed, adding, "Everything east of Nevada is 'back east' to Californians. Ken and I are from San Diego. We're on vacation, too." He smiled at George.

Bess and Jay came over and plunked themselves down onto two chairs. "Whew! What a workout," Bess said.

"Well, I don't know about the rest of you, but I'm going to turn in," Nancy said. "It's nearly midnight, and we had a long drive today."

"Hey, this is the last dance," Bess said, as the music began. "We have to join that one."

Everyone crowded onto the dance floor for a final line dance the instructor called the Earth-

8

quake. By the time they had twisted, turned, and hopped through it, they were weak with laughter.

Then Nancy, George, and Bess said good night to their new friends and headed for the cottage.

"I'm exhausted," Bess said happily as they walked through the dark, fragrant pine grove. "I can't wait to hit that pillow."

Nancy reached into her pocket for the cottage key. "Wait a minute," she said softly as they neared the cottage. "That's odd." She held her arm back to stop the other two.

The small porch light next to the cottage door was on and illuminated the narrow stoop. Nancy held her breath as she noticed that the door was open a crack.

"Be careful," Nancy whispered as they inched slowly forward.

She strained to hear any sound from behind the slightly open cottage door. Her eyes narrowed as she peered through the opening into the dark living room. She reached out with her fingertips and lightly brushed the door. Slowly, it creaked open.

Still holding her breath, Nancy cautiously pushed the cottage door open farther. Behind her, George gasped as the porch light's beam spread across the living room floor to reveal the place in shambles.

2

Hi Ho Bess

"Oh, no," Nancy said. The padded seats of two chairs were ripped and shredded. Their cotton batting spilled and drifted around the room. Kitchen cabinets had been torn and splintered from the wall. The floor was covered with jagged pieces of the linen cabinet and bathroom medicine chest.

Nancy reached around and flipped on the living room light. She waited a few seconds, but there was no activity in the cottage, so she stepped cautiously inside. George followed her, then Bess.

When they were sure no one else was there, Bess ran to the bedroom to check their belongings. A few articles of clothing had been thrown from the closet. Suitcases lay open and had been turned upside down.

10

"I'll call Didi," George offered.

"Good idea," Nancy said. "She'll get the police here in an instant. In the meantime, we can't disturb anything. The police will want everything left just the way we found it."

"Sheriff Jacobs will be here shortly," Didi said breathlessly when she and Mrs. Myers entered the cabin a few minutes later. For a moment she looked as if she was going to cry, then she looked as if she were going to explode. "I'll get him," she said, her voice suddenly low and filled with anger. "This is the final straw."

Nancy, startled at Didi's outburst, began to ask what she meant, but the arrival of Cal and the sheriff interrupted her.

"Looks like someone took an ax to this place," Sheriff Jacobs said, looking around.

"It could have happened anytime between six-thirty and just a few minutes ago," Nancy said. "While we were at the barbecue and the dance."

Everyone nodded except Mrs. Myers. "Actually, I was in here about seven-thirty," she said. "I took away the washcloths and towels and left the girls clean ones."

"And you locked the door when you left?" Sheriff Jacobs asked.

"Of course," Mrs. Myers said, pushing her lower lip out a little. "I didn't notice anything out of place then. Of course I don't make a habit of snooping around the guest quarters."

"Well, the door wasn't jimmied," Sheriff

11

Jacobs said. "So whoever did this used a key to get in."

"We've checked our belongings," Nancy said, nodding to George and Bess. "There doesn't seem to be anything taken, Sheriff."

"I think it's malicious vandalism, pure and simple," Didi said. "Another attempt to run me out. Well, I'm *not* leaving Opa!"

Nancy was surprised at the force of the young woman's anger and made a mental note to ask Didi more about it later.

Didi stalked toward the door. "Come on, girls, gather your things," she said. "I'll find you another cottage."

Sheriff Jacobs began to gather evidence. Cal stayed to help. Didi sent Mrs. Myers to get clean linen, then led Nancy, Bess, and George to another cottage fifty yards away on the same bluff. It was laid out and furnished just like the other one, except the quilts had different patterns.

Didi was shaking while she helped them settle in. "What did you mean by another attempt to run you out?" Nancy asked as she hung her clothes in the roomy closet.

Didi shook her head slightly as Mrs. Myers arrived with fresh linen, indicating to Nancy to be quiet. Nancy understood and asked no further questions. "I'll do the beds," Didi said to Mrs. Myers. "You get on home. It's been a big day."

After the older woman had left, Didi exploded. "I don't know how much more I can

12

take!" she said. Tears welled in her eyes as she whipped a clean sheet over the bed.

Nancy helped Didi tuck in the corners of the sheet, saying, "You seem to have an idea about who is responsible for vandalizing the cottage."

"I *know* who did it," Didi said. "I just can't prove it." She sank to the bed, her face buried in her hands. "It had to be Marco Arias."

"Who is he?" Nancy asked gently, sitting in the small chair opposite Didi.

"Marco Arias and his wife, Martina, own a big dude ranch next to Opa," Didi explained. "They bought all the land behind Opa and turned it into a fancy resort. The only problem is that it's all inland—it doesn't include any oceanfront property. Opa stands between the dude ranch and the bluffs."

Didi wiped her eyes with a tissue, then led the others back into the living room and over to the window. The almost full moon reflected off the water. There was no sign of civilization except the lights of an occasional fishing boat.

"This isn't the first incident at Opa," Didi said. "Marco and his wife have tried everything they can think of. They've accused me of zoning violations, even tax fraud. But none of their nastiness has worked."

She turned back from the window. "They're trying to put me out of business," she said sadly. "Then they can get control of my land and expand the dude ranch to the ocean bluffs. Big Sur has changed since my folks started this place,

13

but there's still a lot of wilderness. Some of it is on Opa. I want to preserve it."

"I thought you were awfully young to be the owner of such a big place," Bess said quietly. "Are your parents gone?"

"Yes," Didi answered. "They died in a plane crash a year ago and left me Opa. I'm twenty and it's quite a job. I'm an only child, and it's just me and Uncle Nick—he's my mother's brother, and he lives in town. He's also my lawyer and the executor of the trust fund my parents set up for me. Opa is my whole life, and I can't lose this place."

Nancy's heart went out to the young woman. Nancy had always felt lucky to have a strong father like Carson Drew to turn to when she needed help or support. "Is there anything we can do?" she asked gently.

"Nancy is a great detective," Bess said eagerly. "She's solved so many cases. I'm sure she could find out who ransacked your cottage."

"I couldn't let you. I've bothered you enough for one night with my problems. You're supposed to be here on vacation," Didi murmured, her head down. She started for the door.

"It's truly no bother," Nancy said. "I'd be happy to look into it, if you'd let me."

Didi let out a big sigh, then turned back from the door. "I'd love it," she said. "I really don't know where to turn for help anymore. Everyone still treats me like a kid. Nobody pays attention to my suspicions of the Ariases, not even Uncle

14

Nick. I need proof. I'd be so grateful for your help. Thank you."

After Didi left, Nancy and her friends talked about the turn of events as they got ready for bed. "I really hope we can do something," George said. "If those Arias people are really trying to run her out of Opa, she needs all the help she can get."

"I know," Nancy said as she started up the loft ladder, "but there's one thing that's bothering me. If someone just wanted to destroy the place, why use a key to get in? Why not tear down the door? And if it was a burglar, why wasn't anything stolen?"

"I'm too tired to think anymore," Bess mumbled from the bedroom. "I'm hitting the hay."

"Good idea," Nancy called from her loft bed. "Sweet dreams, you two." She wanted to think some more about the break-in, but she felt herself drifting off to sleep as she snuggled under the soft quilts.

Wednesday morning dawned gray and drizzly, with a soft rain shimmering on the grass outside the cabin. Nancy, Bess, and George added bulky sweaters to their T-shirts and jeans. After breakfast, they headed into the village of Cliffton, about five miles away. "I just want to get some background to Didi's story," Nancy explained. "Before I rush to someone's rescue, I like to have all the facts."

A quick check in the municipal records office

15

showed that the Arias Dude Ranch had no beach access. Didi had indeed been investigated for zoning violations and tax fraud, but no charges had been filed. Both investigations had been prompted by anonymous tips and not, as Didi had indicated, by Marco and Martina Arias.

After a drive around the village, the three friends decided on a late lunch at a small clifftop restaurant with a gorgeous view of the mountains.

"Didn't we see you at the Opa barbecue last night?" Nancy asked the young waitress when she brought their hamburgers and fries.

"Yeah, I go a couple of times a month," the waitress said. "Better enjoy them while I can. Not sure how much longer they'll be having them."

"What do you mean?" Nancy asked.

"Well, I probably shouldn't say . . ." the waitress began.

"Come on," Bess said. "We won't tell anyone."

"Well, Didi's been having some problems," the waitress said, leaning over their table.

"She's just a kid," the middle-aged cook chimed in from behind the counter. "She grew up at Opa, but that doesn't mean she can run the place. It's hard work."

"Her parents, now, that's a different story," the waitress said. *They* knew how to run Opa."

"Didi seems to be trying to do her best, though, don't you think?" Nancy asked.

"Maybe," the cook said, taking a swipe at the

16

countertop with a damp cloth. "But she's been in hot water off and on. Nothing ever proved, mind you, but trouble nevertheless."

"She's in over her head," the waitress said. "Don't know why she even tries to keep that place going. Her folks left her plenty of money. I'd just live off that and not work at all, if I was her."

"How about the Ariases?" Nancy asked. "What's their dude ranch like?"

"Fancy, fancy," the cook muttered.

"It's okay." The waitress shrugged. "Mostly for rich tourists."

The drizzle had stopped by the time Nancy, Bess, and George finished their lunch, so they strolled down the main street of Cliffton, looking in the windows of the village shops. Nancy and George bought sweatshirts, and Bess bought a pair of riding boots.

"How about giving those new boots a tryout tonight?" George asked her cousin on their drive back to Opa. The sun was beginning to show through the ocean fog. "I'm definitely going on that trail ride down to the beach. You two with me?"

"Sure," Nancy said.

"I guess," Bess said, then added with a good-natured laugh, "but it's a shame to get my new boots dirty by riding."

Because they had had a late lunch, the girls went straight to their cottage and skipped dinner in the lodge. While they put away their pur-

17

chases, Nancy got a call from Didi. She had talked to Sheriff Jacobs about the break-in the night before.

"He thinks there are two possibilities," Didi said. "It was either vandalism by some local kids out to do some mischief. Or it might have been a robbery attempt—someone looking for jewelry or other valuables. He says he has no evidence linking the Ariases to the mess. But I still believe Marco's behind it. Help me prove it, Nancy."

"I'll do my best," Nancy assured her. She told Didi about their trip to Cliffton, without mentioning what the waitress and cook thought about Didi's mismanagement. Finally, she told Didi that she and her friends had decided to take a trail ride down to the beach that evening.

"Good. I hope that will take your mind off this mess," Didi said. "Just go on down to the stable. Cal will fix you right up."

When she hung up, Nancy told Bess and George what Didi had said. "She's really upset," Nancy concluded. "We've got to help her if we can."

"Can we go on our ride first," George asked, "and get back on the case after that?"

"Okay," Nancy said with a smile. "Maybe a trip to the dude ranch would be fun for tomorrow."

Within minutes they had walked to the stable. Cal and his stable hand Barney picked out three horses, saddled them, and helped the girls up. Cal pointed out the beach trail.

They reached the bluff in about twenty minutes. The view was spectacular. The ocean was turning a purplish blue as it got darker. "It looks so mysterious," Bess said with a shiver. Nancy turned to see that behind them, mountains made jagged black silhouettes against the starry sky.

"Be careful," George warned as she started down the cliff trail leading to the beach. "This path is rocky. And it could be slippery from the rain."

Bess's horse followed George's. Then Nancy gently encouraged her horse along the steep path after Bess. He seemed surefooted and comfortable. "I think these guys have been down this trail a few hundred times before," Nancy said. "Let's take it slowly anyway."

"It is kind of steep," Bess said, peering over the edge of the cliff at the waves crashing against the rocks below.

"Don't worry," George called back. "Follow me."

"Maybe we should have taken the canyon trail instead," Bess said nervously.

"This will be worth it when we get to the bottom," Nancy said. "It will be so beautiful."

They continued a few more yards down to the sea. Nancy watched as Bess moved sideways in her saddle. "I can't seem to get comfortable," Bess said. "This saddle keeps slipping."

"Stop complaining and relax," George said. "Honestly—next time we'll just lower you over the side in a bucket."

"Hold on tight to the reins," Nancy said. "The horse knows what to do."

"I'm glad somebody does," Bess muttered. "I'm not too crazy about riding down the side of a cliff."

As the horses cautiously stepped down the trail, Nancy divided her concentration between watching the path and seeing Bess squirm in her saddle. "Try to keep a steady seat, Bess," Nancy said. "Don't move around so much."

"I'm not moving on purpose," Bess called back, her voice trembling. "There's something wrong with my saddle—I just know it. It feels like it's slipping. . . ."

Bess's words trailed off as her saddle slid down over the side of the horse. For a second, Bess hung there in an awkward split, one leg hanging straight down, the other over the horse's back. Then, in one terrifying move, her horse reared up, and Bess and the saddle were flipped away.

In horror, Nancy watched as Bess sailed over the side of the steep cliff, her screams filling the salty night air.

3

Trapped!

As she tumbled over the bluff, Bess grasped frantically at the weeds growing out of the trail. Finally, she grabbed the edge of a large rock with her fingertips. Her body hung high above the dark rocky beach. "Help me!" she cried as she dangled. "Hurry!"

Nancy reined in her horse and scrambled out of the stirrups and onto the ground. She raced toward her friend. "We're coming, Bess," she yelled.

George followed quickly. "Whatever you do, don't let go," she urged.

Nancy reached Bess in seconds and grabbed her wrists firmly. With George's help, she hoisted Bess back up over the edge of the bluff.

Sitting on the trail, Bess struggled to catch her breath but couldn't. She gulped for air, then

21

stammered, "I t-told you we should take the canyon trail."

"Your knee's really banged up," Nancy said, looking at Bess's torn jeans. Underneath the ripped fabric in one knee, Nancy could see that Bess's knee was scraped and swollen.

"My new boots!" Bess said. Scrapes and scratches marred the leather's shiny black finish.

"If she's worried about her boots, she's okay," George said, grinning.

"Just sit there," Nancy said. She looked over the side of the bluff. Bess's saddle was about ten yards down, its strap caught on a sharp rock. Nancy shuddered when she thought of what could have happened to Bess if she'd fallen all the way down.

"Can you see it?" George asked, joining her on the bluff's edge.

"Yes," Nancy answered. "And I think we can get it. Bring over the rope on your saddle, okay?"

"What's going on?" Bess called. "Why aren't we going back? I want to soak in a nice warm tub."

"Just a few more minutes, Bess," Nancy replied as George returned with a large coil of rope. "Lie back and rest for a while. George, can you round up Bess's horse? I saw it heading back up the trail."

George left and Nancy unwound the thick thirty-yard rope. There was a large steel hook on one end. Dangling the rope over the edge of the bluff, she tried to hook it onto the saddle. After a few misses, she finally hooked the rope onto one of the stirrups.

When George returned, they tied the rope to the saddle of her horse. With encouraging words and clucks from Nancy and George, the horse hauled the saddle up and over the edge of the bluff.

"You think someone tampered with the saddle, don't you?" George said. "Someone intentionally—"

"Shhh," Nancy answered softly, looking over the saddle. "I don't want to upset Bess. It's just a hunch, that's all. It's worth checking out after last night's break-in." She carefully examined the broken strap.

"So?" George asked.

"Hmm, I don't know," Nancy said. "This could have been cut, but it's hard to tell. The saddle's pretty old and worn."

"Hey, remember me?" Bess called out. "The one who was nearly killed a little while ago?"

"Sorry, Bess," Nancy said. "We'll go back now."

Nancy placed the saddle on Bess's horse, then tied the horse's reins to her own saddle so she could lead the horse back. Then she helped George hoist Bess up into George's saddle. Bess groaned a little but bravely took the reins.

Then Nancy boosted George up onto the horse's back behind Bess, mounted her own horse, and they rode back to the Opa stable.

Cal called Didi down when he heard what had

happened. Then Didi drove Nancy, Bess, and George back to the cottage in a golf cart.

"Are you sure she's okay?" Didi asked as Bess ran a bath. "I can take her to the doctor."

"I think she's fine," Nancy said, pulling a chair close to the fireplace. "But we'll watch her and see how she is after a good night's sleep."

"Cal should have gone with you," Didi said. "Some of those trails can be rough for beginners."

"I'm *not* a beginner," Bess said sharply as she joined the others. She had put on her sleep shirt and a terry cloth robe. "The problem was my saddle. It was loose or torn."

"I'm so sorry," Didi said, helping Bess to the chair Nancy had prepared with extra cushions. "I'll talk to Cal. I'll have him check all the bridles and saddles personally and make sure there aren't any others with problems. I'm just thankful you're okay," she added. With that, Didi said good night and left the cabin quickly. Nancy could see she was really upset.

"You would tell us if you needed to see a doctor, right?" George asked her cousin as she rubbed Bess's shoulders and neck. "You know, it's not just your knee I'm worried about. Hanging by your arms can really stress out your shoulders."

"I'm fine—no kidding," Bess said. She put her feet up on the stool Nancy had placed in front of her. The fire's embers glowed reddish gold as they talked.

"I'm glad they're checking the rest of the saddles and the other riding equipment," Nancy murmured. "Just in case . . ."

Thursday morning was bright and clear.

"It's a perfect day for a little visit to the Arias Dude Ranch—if you feel up to it," Nancy said, looking at Bess as they sipped their coffee in the living room.

"I feel fine," Bess said, then added with a crooked grin, "just don't make me try out any of their horses."

Nancy telephoned Marco Arias's office while Bess showered and George straightened up the bedroom.

"I got his secretary," Nancy told her friends when she hung up. "She says there's a horse show going on there today. Mr. Arias is emcee-ing. She told me that she's the only one in the office. So I say," she added with a sly grin, "it's a perfect time to visit the dude ranch and have a look around."

By the time they all had dressed, it was mid-morning. They were the last to arrive in the lodge dining room. Mrs. Myers led them to a table on the sunny porch.

They were surprised when Didi brought out their pancakes and sausage herself. "How are you, Bess?" she asked, taking a seat. "Better, I hope."

"I'm still sore," Bess answered, "but okay."

25

"We're planning a field trip today," Nancy said with a smile. "To the Arias Dude Ranch."

"Great!" Didi said. "Get me some proof, Nancy. I know that Arias is trying to ruin me."

They changed the subject when Mrs. Myers arrived with coffee and tea. "That mountain is so beautiful," Bess said, pointing to a sharp peak in the distance. "Does it have a name?"

"It's Pico Cielo," Didi said. "Actually, I own a little piece of it. Part of the mountain is on Opa. Join us for some coffee, Betty." Mrs. Myers got another cup, then took a seat at the table.

"Pico Cielo means Heaven's Peak in Spanish, doesn't it?" George asked.

"That's right," Didi said.

"What's all that white stuff on top?" Bess asked. "It can't be snow, can it?"

"It's lime," Didi said. "It looks like snow, doesn't it? There's a mystery about Pico Cielo." She took a sip of coffee. "Do you have time to hear it?"

"Absolutely," Nancy said, pouring boysenberry syrup on her pancakes.

"Well, there was quite a gold rush in this area at the end of the nineteenth century," Didi said. "A miner named Hubbard Wilson worked the land near Pico Cielo from the mid-1880s until after 1900. On his deathbed, he told a fantastic tale."

"Fantastic is right," Mrs. Myers added.

"He said that one day he was hacking away at Pico Cielo and his pickax broke through," Didi continued. "Inside was an amazing cave system dating back to prehistoric times."

"I've heard of caves like that," Nancy said, "especially in areas with heavy lime deposits."

"Here's the really exciting part," Didi said, setting down her coffee cup. "It's said that the caves were filled with streams and ponds that held glowing fish and lizards. There were also insects. These were creatures that had never seen light."

"Wow," Bess said, shivering. "I can't imagine never seeing the sun or feeling its warmth. How could they live without it?"

"It's possible," Nancy said. "These creatures have been found in other caves."

"Has anyone else seen this cave besides Hubbard Wilson?" George asked.

"No," Mrs. Myers said emphatically. "There's a new expedition leaving all the time. It's sort of like the hunt for the Loch Ness monster or the Abominable Snowman. No one has ever found it."

"I'll bet the search for Hubbard's cave is a lot more exciting than some of the other legends," Nancy pointed out. "After all, he was a miner."

"Exactly," Didi said with a nod. "A lot of people don't care about the prehistoric cave itself. There's another part to the legend. People say that Hubbard found gold in the mines around here. Since there was no gold found in his cabin when he died, many people feel that he hid the gold in the cave."

"If he ever found any," Mrs. Myers said. "When you've lived around these parts as long as I have, you hear a lot of things." She pushed a strand of hair off her forehead. "There's a new legend springing up every year."

The five women sat in silence for a few minutes. "Well, I guess we'll go," Nancy said, taking a final sip of tea. "We have a big day ahead of us."

"Make it a good one," Didi said. "I can't wait to hear about it."

Within minutes Nancy, Bess, and George were on their way to the Arias Dude Ranch.

"That prehistoric cave sounds pretty weird, doesn't it?" Bess said. "Strange bugs and fish."

"Not to mention hidden gold," George added.

"Mrs. Myers didn't seem to believe any gold exists. She did say lots of people have tried to find the cave, though," Nancy said. "I'll bet more of them were looking for the gold than for the prehistoric creatures. Maybe we'll have time to check it out ourselves while we're here."

It was a short drive to the dude ranch. As they approached, it was clear to Nancy, Bess, and George that this resort was different from Opa. Slick and modern signs led them along the way and announced the activities and facilities of the ranch ahead.

At last they saw the sign announcing they had arrived. "Mr. Arias's secretary said everyone would be at the horse show," Nancy said. "You two get her out of the building. I'll slip inside the office," Nancy said as she drove through the open gate.

"We can't make it too much of a problem or she'll call for help," George said. "We don't want to interrupt the horse show."

Nancy followed the signs to the administration building and parked in the lot. They all took a few minutes to look around.

"See those bushes there by the corner of the building?" Bess said. "We'll tell the secretary that we heard puppies crying in those bushes. We'll say that we think a dog abandoned her babies. We can act afraid of what might happen to the puppies so near to the parking lot."

"Sounds good," Nancy said. "Take her over to the bushes and I'll sneak in."

"What if someone comes back and you're still in there?" George asked.

"We'll have a signal," Nancy said. "One of you start whistling something."

"How about the River Heights High School fight song?" Bess suggested. "No one but us would know that song so far from home."

"Perfect." Nancy nodded with a grin.

George and Bess went in the front door, and Bess popped back out immediately. "You were right," she said. "There's a big lobby area and a hall leading off it. All the offices open off the hall."

Nancy followed Bess back in, found the women's rest room, and ducked inside. It was empty. She stood inside the door and cracked it open just enough to watch George and Bess go into one of the offices. She heard their voices, then another woman's voice.

At last all three emerged. "Puppies!" the woman said. "I wonder if they're Matilda's. She's been acting kind of odd lately."

"I'm so worried about them, Carol," Bess said.

They bustled through the lobby and out the door. Nancy waited a moment, then raced down the hall to the office the others had left. The first room had the secretary's desk. A sign on the door at the back announced Mr. Arias's office.

Nancy tried the door and it opened. Inside was a very modern, very neat executive office. Plush leather furniture, oil paintings, and a thick carpet were signs of the ranch's success.

Not touching anything, Nancy gazed at the few papers lying on the desk and the credenza behind it. They seemed to be routine lists of food and linen orders. There were three other doors leading from this office. One opened to a private rest room, one to a closet, and one to a conference room.

Nancy was drawn immediately to a scale model of the ranch on a table beneath the conference room window.

As she approached it, she heard a man's voice in the hallway outside the room. "Carol?" the voice called out. "Carol, where are you?"

Frantically, Nancy looked around. There was

no place to hide. She raced back into Mr. Arias's office.

"Carol, this show is great," the man called out. "I want you to close up shop here and come on down with the rest of us. You shouldn't miss this."

Nancy's breath caught in her throat. She dashed for the closet and stepped inside, closing the door quietly. From the crack around the hinge, she could see out into the room.

Nancy's knees trembled as the office door burst open. "Carol? Are you in here?" the man yelled.

The man strode around the desk. Every step brought him nearer to the closet. Nancy clasped her hand over her mouth, so he wouldn't hear her breathing.

The man moved closer and reached for the closet doorknob. Her heart pounding in her throat, Nancy ducked behind the hanging clothes and pressed herself against the back wall of the closet. At that moment the door opened with a rush of air.

4

Eavesdropping on Danger?

A long arm reached into the closet and yanked a fringed vest off a hanger. Then the door slammed shut again. Nancy heard only her pounding pulse and the jingle of the hangers.

Finally, she heard the footsteps move away. It sounded as if the man had gone into the secretary's office. Nancy gasped for air. Still trembling, she listened at the door. She wanted to be sure the man was gone before she left her hiding place.

A door closed in the distance. Nancy thought it was probably the door from the secretary's office into the hall. Then it was silent again.

Nancy waited for a few moments, then eased open the closet door. The door from Mr. Arias's office to the secretary's had been left open. But there was no one in either office.

Suddenly, Nancy heard the familiar strains of the River Heights High School fight song. It was faint at first but grew louder. She closed the closet door again and stood quietly inside.

The hall door leading to the secretary's office opened again. The whistling stopped, but Nancy heard the voices of the man, the secretary Carol, and George.

"I can't imagine what happened to the puppies," George said. "It sounded as if there were at least six or seven."

"The mother probably came back and moved them," Carol said. "At least I hope so."

"Me, too," Bess's voice piped up. "That's why I was whistling. I always whistle when I'm nervous or upset. And I am worried about those puppies."

"Well, I'm sure they're all right," the man said. Nancy watched them through the crack in the door. "Are you girls guests here?" the man asked. "I don't believe I've seen you around."

"No," George said quickly. "We were thinking about coming here next month. We stopped by to look around and find out your rates."

"Come on down to the horse show," the man said. "My wife, Martina, would be happy to show you around when it's over. That's why I'm here, Carol. Close up the office and come on down. I don't want you to miss it."

"Great!" Carol said. Nancy heard the secretary open and shut a desk drawer.

"I'd like to freshen up," George said, loud

enough for Nancy to hear. "We'll be down in a few minutes."

"Fine," the man said pleasantly. "Just follow your ears."

Nancy heard some moving about, then footsteps leaving the office. The door swooshed shut and the room was very quiet.

Nancy waited three full minutes before leaving the closet. She tiptoed across Mr. Arias's office, and then through the secretary's office. She opened the door and peered out into the hall. It was empty. She darted down the hall to the women's rest room and slipped inside.

George and Bess were waiting for her.

Bess slumped back against the wall when she saw Nancy. "Oh, I'm so glad to see you. We didn't know where you were."

Nancy told them about her close call in the closet. Then George told her that she and Bess were looking through the bushes when Mr. Arias surprised them. "We didn't know he'd already been in the office," Bess added.

"Let's just go back to Opa," Bess said. "My knee hurts and I'm hungry."

The three left the building, ran to the car, and left the Arias Dude Ranch. When they got back to Opa, Didi was waiting for them.

"Well?" she said. "What happened?" She hustled Nancy, George, and Bess onto the dining deck and served them tuna sandwiches and iced tea.

Nancy, Bess, and George told their parts of the story. When they finished, Didi smiled, but she was clearly disappointed. "So you didn't find out anything," she said sadly.

"I'm very interested in the scale model of the dude ranch that I saw in the conference room," Nancy said. "I didn't get a chance to look at it closely. But I think the borders of the dude ranch stretched all the way to the ocean."

"They couldn't have," Didi said. "I told you that Opa stands between the dude ranch and the ocean bluffs."

"That's why I want to get a better look," Nancy said. "I have to get back there. Maybe it's a model of his next expansion. If so, he seems to be including the property that Opa is on. I wonder what makes him so sure that he'll get it."

"He'll never get it," Didi said. "Not as long as I'm alive."

It was quiet for a while as Nancy and her friends munched on their sandwiches. Finally, Didi spoke again. "Oh, I have a message for George and Bess. Jay Webb and Ken Randell are down at the tennis courts. They'd like you to join them."

"Right now?" Bess asked.

"They said they'd be there all afternoon," Didi replied. "Bess, do you think you're up to it?"

"Sure," Bess said. "I'm definitely better now that I've rested."

"I'm so glad to hear that," Didi said. "I was

really worried. I've been thinking about your accident, and I want to make it up to you. I'd like to offer you all two complimentary nights at Opa. If you can stay longer this time, wonderful. If not, I'll give you gift certificates. You can use them anytime."

"That's great," Bess said. "Thanks."

"Nancy, I know you've been pretty busy," Didi said, "but I don't suppose you've found out anything yet about who destroyed Hubbard's cottage, have you?"

"Hubbard Wilson?" Nancy said. "You mean our old cottage? The one that was vandalized Tuesday night?"

"Yes," Didi said. "Didn't I tell you that was originally Hubbard's place?"

"No, you didn't," Nancy said. "And you're right. I haven't found out anything about the break-in yet."

"Hubbard Wilson," Bess said. "You mean the miner from the Pico Cielo legend? He was a guest here?"

"No," Didi said. "He lived here. He home-steaded this whole area, including what is now Opa. The guest cottage that was broken into was originally his mining shack. It was remodeled by my folks when they first started up Opa. I had it worked on again after the last earthquake damaged it. But a lot of it is still the way it was when he lived there."

"Earthquake!" Bess said with a shudder.

"Hey, this is California," Didi said with a grin,

shrugging her shoulders. "Earthquakes happen all the time."

"Did Hubbard Wilson build the shack himself?" Nancy asked.

"We're pretty sure he did," Didi answered. "Most of those miners built their own houses. And Hubbard had quite a reputation for cabinet-making. We know he did all the cupboards and woodworking in the cottage because he signed them."

"And now all that work is ruined," George said.

"Pretty much," Didi said. "But there are other examples of his cabinetry around. Some in the village. He also did some work in the most famous house in Big Sur, in fact—it's a mansion called Cloud Palace."

"Our travel brochure mentioned it," Bess said. "We want to go there while we're here."

"Supposedly, Hubbard quit mining after 1900 to work for three years on construction at the palace."

"Why don't we run down there Sunday?" Nancy suggested to her friends.

"Sounds wonderful," George said. Bess nodded her agreement.

"Just so you're here Saturday for our annual Greek Festival," Didi said. "The weather's supposed to be perfect. I'd better get to the kitchen, by the way. Mrs. Myers and I have a lot of work to do."

Didi got up, then turned back. "Nancy, we're

having a final planning meeting for the festival at four o'clock today," she said. "If you'd like to sit in, we'd love to have you. You can see how we operate. Uncle Nick will be there. I'd like you to meet him." Didi looked sad as she gazed at the brook tumbling down from the canyon. "I don't know what I'd do without him."

"I'll be there," Nancy said. "I'd also like a key to Hubbard's old cottage—the one that was vandalized. I'd like to look around in there, if you don't mind."

"No problem," Didi said. "I'll give it to you at the meeting. See you." She walked quickly back to the herb garden, where Mrs. Myers was gathering leaves and twigs.

"A business meeting on your vacation." Bess sighed, as she, Nancy, and George walked to the tennis courts. "What a bore."

"I know," Nancy said. "But I'll get an idea about how things are run around here. Maybe it will help in the investigation."

"Isn't that a coincidence that Hubbard Wilson used to live in the cottage that was vandalized?" George pointed out.

"Maybe a little too much of a coincidence," Nancy said. "Suppose the vandal also knew whose cottage it once was? Maybe he—or she—was after clues to the whereabouts of Hubbard's gold."

"You know, when Didi was telling us all about the caves, it's weird that she didn't tell us that we

38

were in the Hubbard cabin," George said. "The one that was ransacked."

"She has so much to think about," Bess said. "I think she just forgot to tell us."

The threesome arrived at the tennis courts. Bess and George joined Ken and Jay on the court. Nancy watched the tennis match for a while, then took a walk along the stream that bubbled down through the canyon. At four o'clock, she reported to the main lodge building.

"Didi's in her apartment," Mrs. Myers said, nodding toward a door behind the registration desk. "She'll be right out. Why don't you go ahead to the party room. There are refreshments there—just help yourself."

Nancy joined maintenance man Sam Shaw and a few people she didn't know in the party room. Cal and Barney soon arrived from the stables. When Mrs. Myers joined them, she introduced Nancy to the others. Most of the people were from Cliffton or neighboring towns and had been hired to help with the festival. Others were vendors who would run the many booths.

Didi arrived, escorted by a middle-aged man who had her dark, flashing eyes and same good looks. "For those of you who have not met him, this is my uncle, Nick Prenopoulos," Didi said with an affectionate smile. "Nick's my financial advisor. He's going to sit in on today's meeting."

The meeting began smoothly. Nancy learned

that there would be booths selling Greek food, jewelry, and other items. A live band would provide music for dancing, and a small area would be set aside for an outdoor coffee-house. They expected a few thousand people to attend.

After the meeting, everyone left to work on their individual festival assignments. Nancy wandered around the lodge building, winding up on the lower level. She poked around the rooms down there—maintenance room, laundry room, storage and supply rooms.

She checked out a small fitness room at the end of the hall. It was outfitted with the standard workout machines. Doors on one side of the room opened to a sauna and showers. A sliding door on the other side led to a sunny patio.

A large bumblebee buzzed past Nancy's nose, and she realized that the sliding screen to the patio was open a few inches. As she approached the screen to close it, she heard someone talking outside. It was a man and he was obviously very upset.

She poked her head through the open screen and saw Nick Prenopoulos. He was talking into a cellular phone and pacing back and forth on the patio. Nancy popped her head back inside the fitness room before he saw her.

"I tell you, you'll get your money," she heard him say as she listened at the door.

"And you know I've got plenty to back that

up," he continued. "My sister and her husband made a big mistake giving Opa to my niece instead of me. But it's a mistake that's going to be fixed. Opa was always supposed to be mine—and it will be. No matter what it takes!"

5

A Sizzling Dive

Nancy felt a sinking sensation in her stomach. It had been so clear to her by the way Didi had introduced her uncle that Didi loved him very much and trusted him completely. Nancy was now shocked to hear him speak with such bitterness. He was obviously angry about not inheriting Opa.

At last it was quiet. She heard no more words or pacing footsteps from the patio. Cautiously, she peered around the corner of the screen. Nick Prenopoulos was gone.

Nancy hurried down the hall and back up the stairs to the main lobby of the lodge. Her mind was racing. Should I tell Didi what I overheard, she wondered. Or should I find more evidence first? What if Didi's Uncle Nick is behind all the problems at Opa, not Marco Arias?

As she crossed the parking lot and headed for her cottage, Nancy watched Didi hug her uncle before he climbed into his low-slung red sports car and drove away. Didi gave Nancy a cheery wave before going back into the lodge.

I've got to think this through. I've got to be sure before I say anything to Didi.

When Nancy got back to the cottage, Bess was getting up from a nap. George was at the small desk, addressing postcards. Nancy quickly told them about the meeting and what she had heard Didi's uncle say.

"I'm going to call Dad," Nancy concluded. "He can check out Nick Prenopoulos for us." Nancy's father, Carson Drew, was a well-respected lawyer who always had good advice to give. Nancy knew she could turn to him for help on any case. "Didi's uncle is also a lawyer, so they probably have some mutual friends," she added as she dialed her father's number.

Carson Drew wasn't at home, but Nancy left a detailed message on the family's answering machine. Nancy was ready to check out the vandalized cottage. She grabbed the keys that Didi had loaned her and picked up a flashlight, and the three set out along the bluff trail.

Nancy, Bess, and George walked quickly down the path back to the first cottage they had been assigned. Nancy shivered as she remembered finding the destruction just two days earlier.

When they arrived, they saw that the windows

were boarded over. Didi had told her that no one had cleaned up inside yet.

There was a padlock on the door as well as a sign that said Crime Scene—Do Not Enter. Nancy used the keys that Didi had given her to open first the padlock, then the cottage door.

"Now, be careful," Nancy warned them. "There's a lot of broken glass, jagged wood, and nails lying around. We already have our quota of scrapes and cuts for this vacation."

Furniture was still overturned and closets emptied. Hubbard Wilson's beautifully crafted bookshelves, kitchen cabinets, and bathroom cupboards were smashed on the living room floor. Spiders had already begun trailing webs across the rubble.

"Look," Nancy pointed out. "The cabinets and shelving are really torn apart."

"The things that Hubbard made himself," George observed.

"Right," Nancy said. "I'm sure that whoever broke in here knew this was Hubbard Wilson's cottage."

Carefully, the three friends picked through the mess. At last Nancy found something. "Look at this," she cried. "It's a moving panel!"

She held up a chunk of wood, which was the bottom third of a cabinet. A pretty border of hand-carved branches and leaves trailed around the edge, leading to the trunk of the tree in one corner. A fat bear climbed halfway up the trunk.

When Nancy touched the bear's paw, it moved

down like a tiny lever. This tripped a spring in the bottom of the cabinet, revealing a hidden compartment.

"Wow," Bess said. "Hubbard Wilson was pretty clever."

"Did the vandal know about this?" Nancy wondered aloud. "And if so, did he or she take whatever Hubbard hid in that compartment?"

They spent about an hour in the cottage but turned up no more clues. They finally left to go back to their place.

"It was so creepy in there," Bess said. "Let's go for a nighttime swim."

"Sounds like a good idea," George agreed. "How about you, Nancy?"

"You two go ahead and get changed," Nancy said. "I want to show this to Didi. I'll be back in a minute."

They parted on the path, and Nancy continued on to the main lodge. She found Didi and Mrs. Myers in Didi's office.

"We were going over the menu for the weekend," Didi said. "What have you got there?"

Nancy showed the two women the cabinet piece. She tripped the lever that opened the compartment.

"My word," Mrs. Myers said. "All these years and I never noticed it. Are you sure it's really a hiding place? Those cabinets were practically destroyed. Maybe it was broken and just looks like a hidden compartment."

"No, I think Nancy's right," Didi said, turning

45

the piece of wood over in her hand. "That's fantastic," she said to Nancy. "I knew it was a good idea to put you on the case."

"Thanks," Nancy said. "But it's just a start. Have you heard anything more from the sheriff?"

"He called this morning," Didi said. "He doesn't really have any suspects. He still thinks it might have been kids out for a little mischief. There are a few that he knows about that have been in trouble for this kind of thing before."

"Did they find any fingerprints?" Nancy asked. "That would be a pretty quick way to see if it was these same kids or not."

"They found some." Didi nodded. "But they were mostly Opa staff people. They also found a few smudged ones. Of course, the ones that weren't Opa employees could have come from someone who stayed in the cottage. We don't fingerprint our guests. None of the prints matched any locally known criminals."

"Since nothing was stolen, nothing can be traced," Nancy said. "That's going to make this mystery difficult to solve."

"I know you can do it," Didi said with a smile. "You've just got to. You're all I have. No one else believes me."

Nancy thought about what she had heard Didi's uncle say. Perhaps her new friend was even more alone than she knew.

"I'd like to keep this piece of wood a while longer," Nancy said, "if you don't mind."

"Sure," Didi said.

"Well, Bess and George and I are going for an evening swim," Nancy said. "We'll see you at breakfast tomorrow."

Nancy went back to her cottage, changed into her swimsuit, and she and her friends started their walk up the path to the hilltop pool. Halfway up, Nancy thought she heard a sound in the woods. The hairs on her arms bristled.

Nancy held back while Bess and George went ahead. She stopped and looked around, but saw nothing in the dense woods but gray-green darkness. Walking slowly, she strained her ears for sounds.

Finally, she caught up with George and Bess. When they reached the pool area at the top of the small hill, Nancy looked around again.

Ahead, the bluffs dropped to the dark, crashing sea. The mountains behind jutted blue-black into the starry sky. The stream tumbled down a canyon and wound around the pool.

"Maybe it's too chilly for a swim," Bess said with a shudder. She wrapped her towel around her shivering body.

"Not for me," George said enthusiastically. "It's perfect." She hurried ahead and eagerly scrambled onto the diving board.

Nancy and Bess watched as George did a few stretching exercises. Then she bounced a couple of times, testing the spring of the diving board. She flashed a broad grin to her friends and inched her toes to the front edge of the board.

As George raised her arms high over her head,

a peculiar sound drew Nancy's attention to the sky. At first she didn't realize what she was seeing. It looked like a long, looping snake flying through the air.

Then, in a chilling moment, Nancy understood. It was the cable from the television satellite tower, and one end was disconnected. The cable was drifting down toward the pool, carrying enough electricity to fry anything in the water.

"George!" Nancy yelled as her friend bounced high in the air off the diving board. "Don't dive!"

6

Two Plus Two Make Five

George's head whipped around to look at Nancy. She had a startled expression on her face, and her body seemed to hang in the air for a moment. As she came back down, she grabbed clumsily for the end of the diving board. Her feet hung a foot above the water.

Nancy ran to the edge of the board and grabbed George just as the end of the cable dropped into the pool with an electrifying crackle. Nancy held on tightly to her friend as George's legs dangled above the sizzling water.

Nancy helped George back onto the diving board. They sat there for a minute catching their breath.

"George! Nancy!" Bess called from the safe ground next to the pool. "Are you all right? George—you could have been killed!"

"I'm okay," George said, rubbing her shoulder. "Thanks to Nancy."

Nancy and George plopped down next to Bess on the grass beside the pool. "A cable break—what a horrible accident," Bess said, giving her cousin a big hug.

"If it *was* an accident," Nancy said, frowning as she stared into the steaming pool.

"Nancy, you don't think—" George started.

"—that someone cut that cable on purpose," Bess finished.

"I'm not sure," Nancy said. "I heard something in the woods as we were walking up the path."

"This is pretty wild country," Bess pointed out, looking around nervously. "Maybe it was an animal—a bear or a mountain lion. Come to think of it, that's a pretty scary thought itself."

"So you think it was more sabotage against Opa?" George asked.

"Maybe," Nancy said, frowning.

"Perhaps Didi is right," Bess said. "Maybe it *is* Marco Arias—and he'll do anything to get Opa."

"What are you thinking about, Nancy?" George asked.

"We've been here only two days, right?" Nancy said. "Our cottage has been broken into, Bess has been pitched over a bluff, and now this. It seems to be more personal than just sabotage of Opa."

"You mean *we're* the targets?" Bess asked. "Now you're really scaring me."

50

"Even so, it still could be Mr. Arias," George said. "We never went down to the horse show. Maybe he suspects something."

"If you're right," Bess said, her voice wavering, "he's more dangerous than we thought."

"If someone is aiming these events directly at us," Nancy pointed out, "it has to be someone with easy access to Opa. I'm not sure that Marco Arias could come and go without being noticed."

"He could sneak through the woods," George said. "His land borders on Opa's boundaries."

"Well, whoever it is, why would he—or she—come after us?" Bess wondered.

"Maybe someone knows we're looking into the sabotage," Nancy said, "and wants us to stop."

"Or thinks we've discovered something already," George said. "But what?"

"That's what we need to find out," Nancy said.

Nancy and her friends walked back down to the stable. Without going into detail about George's near miss, Nancy reported the broken cable to Didi, Cal, and Barney, who were brushing down the horses.

"Something probably chewed through the cable," Sam said.

"A wild animal?" Bess asked.

"That happens up here sometimes," Cal said with a frown. "A squirrel or a raccoon. We'll get an electrician out tomorrow to take a look."

"Thank goodness none of you were in the pool when it happened," Didi said.

Nancy and her friends headed back to their

51

cottage. Didi walked partway with them. "You three are still planning to come to the festival Saturday, I hope," Didi said.

"Wouldn't miss it," Nancy assured her.

"Good," Didi said. "It's the thirtieth Greek Festival at Opa, and it should be our best ever. People come from miles around. Hey, if you haven't got anything planned for tomorrow, why don't you come up into the canyons with us."

They paused at the turnoff where the path branched in two directions. "Cal and I are going to gather wildflowers and vines. Betty makes the most beautiful decorations out of them. She does that every year for the festival."

Nancy looked at Bess and George, who nodded. "Sounds good to us," Nancy said. "We were planning a canyon hike sometime during our stay."

"Great," Didi said as she started toward the main lodge. "I'll see you after breakfast."

When they got back to their cottage, George headed for the shower. Bess fixed them all a snack. Nancy looked around carefully. She didn't want to alarm her friends, but she couldn't shake the feeling that someone had been in their cottage while they were gone. If so, what was the intruder looking for?

After tossing and turning, Nancy finally fell into a fitful sleep.

* * *

On Friday morning Nancy was awakened by the ringing of the phone on the small nightstand next to her bed.

"Dad!" she said. "Do you have some information for me?"

"I sure do," Carson Drew answered. "It seems your suspicions about Didi's uncle might be right. Nick Prenopoulos has quite a reputation."

"For what?" Nancy said. She sat up quickly in the bed, her senses alert.

"Gambling," her father told her. "He's what they call a real high roller. He spends a lot of time in Las Vegas, Reno, and Lake Tahoe—and all of that time is spent gambling."

"Does he make a lot of money at it?" Nancy asked.

"Once in a while," her father said. "Most of the time he loses, but he just keeps gambling."

"Which means that he has to come up with more money to bet, right?" Nancy said.

"I'm afraid so," Carson Drew agreed.

"Dad, he sounded so desperate and angry when I overheard him on the phone. Maybe he's the one who's trying to get control of Opa. That way he can sell it—maybe even to Marco Arias. And then he'd have plenty of money to gamble with."

"Until he loses that, too," Mr. Drew said.

"I wonder if Didi knows about his gambling," Nancy said. "It might be a terrible blow."

"Move slowly," her father warned. "Make sure of your facts. I'll call if I hear anything else."

Nancy wondered if she should tell him what had happened at the pool the night before. She decided it might worry him too much, so she didn't say anything.

She woke Bess and George and told them what her father had said. Then they dressed in jeans, shirts, and hiking shoes. George and Nancy tied jackets around their waists. Bess grabbed a sweater.

When they finished breakfast, Didi met them and they went to the stable to pick up Cal.

"I'm glad you brought jackets," Didi said. "It can get kind of cool in the canyons. You're going to get quite a guided tour today. Cal's hobbies are botany, archaeology, paleontology—all the natural sciences."

"Is he from the Big Sur area?" Nancy asked.

"No," Didi answered, "Montana. But he knows more about this country around here than I do."

Cal drove the pickup truck on the two-lane coast road that spanned the Big Sur area. They passed an odd assortment of houses—rickety old miner's shacks, farmhouses, redwood cabins, and dazzling glass-and-wood showplaces.

Finally, the truck turned off the main highway and started up a dirt road into one of the high mountain canyons that was part of Opa.

"This road could use a little work," George said as they bounced from side to side.

"It's an old logging road," Didi said. "Can you imagine what it was like when the first settlers came here? They had nothing but horse trails up the mountains and down to the sea."

"Actually, I can imagine just what it was like," Bess said, rubbing her knee.

"That's right, you can," Didi said, with a smile. "Sorry about that."

Cal parked the car, and they all piled out, carrying baskets and boxes, shears and clippers. Nancy felt the dampness of the air on her cheeks. "Is that a redwood?" she asked Cal, pointing ahead.

"It sure is," he answered. "It's more than three hundred feet high and maybe eight hundred years old."

"It looks like it's been here forever," George said, bending her head way back to look toward the top of the majestic tree.

"Actually, ten to fifteen million years ago, the ground we're walking on wasn't even here," Cal said. "The coastline was several miles farther east. All this area was created by earthquakes pushing the earth out toward the ocean."

As they walked along a rough trail, Cal pointed out other trees and plants. Occasionally, a broad beam of sunlight would pierce the heavy growth of the forest. Overhead, a golden eagle circled slowly.

"We're almost there," Didi said after a half-hour hike. She smiled and her eyes twinkled as if she was about to share a secret.

They left the trail, walking on a spongy carpet

of moss. Finally, they pushed through a grove of fir trees and stepped into a small open meadow.

"Oh, wow," Nancy said with a sigh. The sunlight turned the field of wildflowers into glowing bright lights—pink and red poppies, orange paintbrush, and yellow wild mustard. Around these were thousands of lupine in tall spikes of purple, white, blue, and yellow. It was a dazzling sight.

Cal and Didi showed Nancy, George, and Bess what and where to pick and cut and soon their baskets were full of wildflowers. Dozens of hummingbirds darted in and out of the bright blossoms. A butterfly balanced on Nancy's hand as she reached for a golden poppy.

Didi and Bess went into the woods to cut ferns. Nancy and George helped Cal with the wild vines he had clipped. "Didi told us that your hobby is the natural sciences," Nancy said to Cal.

"Yes," he said. "It started when I was a child in Montana. I was a fossil nut and a real rock hound—had my own tools and polisher."

Didi and Bess returned, nearly hidden by the ferns heaped in their boxes. "So what do you think?" Didi asked. "Do we have enough?"

"This ought to do it," Cal said. He piled the overflowing baskets and boxes onto long coils and loops of vines. Then, using the vines as a sort of sled, they dragged the whole load back down the canyon.

When they arrived at the truck, they carefully

dunked the flowers and plants in the large tubs of water that Cal had placed in the truck bed.

When the group returned to Opa, Cal unloaded the boxes and baskets. Then he drove to the stable.

While Nancy and her friends helped sort the flowers, Jay and Ken stopped by to challenge Bess and George to another tennis match. Nancy urged them to go ahead, saying she'd come down to the courts to cheer them on later. Meanwhile, she wanted to do a little more investigating.

"I'd like to check some of your records," she explained to Didi, "especially the claims and charges that Marco Arias made against you and Opa."

"We can easily do that," Didi assured her. She took Nancy into her office and turned on her computer. Then she typed in her password and called up Opa's files.

"I have a separate file for my dealings with Marco," Didi said.

As Nancy scanned the names and dates, Didi was called away to greet the people who were selling T-shirts at the festival. "Nancy, can you manage by yourself here for a little while?" Didi asked. "These are some of my best vendors. I want to keep them happy."

"Sure," Nancy said. "No problem."

"I'll be back in a half hour or so," Didi said. "If you finish before then, just lock up when you leave." She left the office, closing the door behind her.

With Didi gone, Nancy was free to explore the financial records of Opa more closely. She soon discovered that Didi was right—it had not been a good year.

Nancy then checked the file drawer in the desk. It was locked, but she was able to open it with the penknife she carried in her bag.

There were just a few files—mostly accounts from the days when Didi's parents were alive.

In the back of the file drawer were copies of records for the trust fund Didi's parents had set up. Nancy scanned the accounts and recognized immediately that something wasn't right.

"That's odd," she mumbled to herself. She rechecked the numbers from the past year. Why would the trust fund lend Opa three thousand dollars for flowers for the Greek Festival. I thought we picked all the flowers that were going to be used, Nancy thought.

She checked back with Opa's financial records on the computer. There was no entry for the loan. As she looked further, she had more questions. Her heart racing, she quickly printed out some of the questionable records and slipped them in her bag.

Then she took the trust file over to the photocopy machine in the corner and made copies of some of the pages. She knew she had to be quick. Didi could return any minute. As the fresh copies drifted out onto the holding tray, she heard footsteps in the hall. They were heading right for the door to Didi's office.

"Come on," Nancy muttered to the copy machine. "Hurry up!" Her heart pounding, she fed the final page into the machine as the doorknob clicked.

"No, thank you, Mrs. Myers," a voice called out from the other side of the office door. "I'll just be a minute."

Nancy recognized the voice. It was Nick Prenopoulos—and he was opening the office door.

7

Ambush!

When the last page emerged from the copy machine, Nancy ran back to the desk and added the copies to the printouts already in her bag.

She slipped the files back in the drawer. It relocked automatically. She closed out the computer files just as Nick Prenopoulos opened the door.

"What are you doing in here?" he asked, scowling. He walked to the desk and glanced around as if to make sure she hadn't stolen anything. He rested his hand on the back of the computer.

Nancy knew the computer was still warm. Her mind raced for an answer in case he asked her why she was there. She knew Didi's uncle was smart and couldn't be fooled easily.

She took a deep breath. "Didi asked me to

check something on her computer," she said. "I was just leaving." She started around the desk.

Mr. Prenopoulos narrowed his eyes as he studied her.

"Uncle Nick, there you are." With the welcome sound of Didi's voice, Nancy let out a huge sigh. Mr. Prenopoulos softened his expression a little.

"Hi, Didi," Nancy said. "Your computer is great. Well, I'd better join Bess and George at the tennis courts." She gave them both a big smile, then walked out of the office.

Outside, Nancy took another deep breath, then headed for the tennis courts. When the match was over, Jay and Ken gave her a wave and left. Bess and George joined Nancy.

"Those guys are so cool," Bess said. "They're going to sit with us at the campfire supper tonight. Speaking of food, I'm starved!" Bess said, wiping her brow with a towel. "I don't know whether you two noticed, but somehow we missed lunch."

"We've got snacks back in the cottage," Nancy said. "Let's eat there—I want to show you two something."

Back in their little kitchen, George made cheese sandwiches while Bess poured sodas and opened a bag of chips. Nancy studied the pages she had printed and copied in Didi's office. She showed them to her friends when they gathered around the table.

"Look," she said, pointing to a column of

entries. "The records for the trust fund show that several large amounts were taken out," Nancy said. "All that money was supposed to go into Opa to help overcome the losses the resort has had."

"That should help a lot," Bess said. "Didi's lucky to have it."

Nancy pointed to another page. "But look here," she continued. "These are the financial records for Opa for last year. That money never made it into the Opa account. We're talking about nearly a hundred thousand dollars."

"What do you suppose happened to it?" Bess asked.

"I don't think Didi can blame Mr. Arias for that," George added.

"The question is, does she know about it at all," Nancy said. "Remember what the people at that restaurant said. Didi doesn't exactly have a head for business. If she depends on her uncle to manage the trust, she might not double-check any records."

"So you think he's taking the money for himself," George said.

"Maybe," Nancy said, "to support his gambling."

"What if Didi does know about it?" Bess said. "And she's keeping quiet to protect her uncle."

"I'd hate to think that was true," Nancy said grimly.

"But what about the rest of it?" Bess wondered. "The sabotage and all that. Do you think he's to blame for that, too?"

"I don't know," Nancy said. "He did say that Opa would be his soon. Maybe he and Mr. Arias are working together. First Opa goes under and Uncle Nick convinces Didi to sell it to Mr. Arias. Then Mr. Arias gives Uncle Nick a kickback for arranging the sale—enough to replace the money embezzled from the trust fund."

"Maybe it's time to have a talk with Mr. Arias," Nancy said, reaching for the phone. She called the dude ranch and said she was in the area to choose a place for a large corporate retreat to be held the following spring.

"I'm getting a full tour in half an hour," she told Bess and George when she hung up. "And it will be personally guided by Mrs. Martina Arias!"

Since Mr. Arias and his secretary would recognize Bess and George, the three decided that Nancy would go alone. Nancy changed to a skirt, jacket, and heels, and drove the Mustang the short distance to the dude ranch.

Mrs. Arias was waiting in the lobby of the administration building. She was dressed in a denim skirt and blouse with a silver concho belt. Her bright red hair spilled out from under a white cowgirl hat that matched her boots.

"We're so pleased you're considering our ranch," she said to Nancy as she escorted her to a golf cart. The grand tour took over an hour, during which Mrs. Arias kept up a constant patter of statistics and details. Nancy dutifully wrote down the facts in the notebook she had brought.

They finally returned to the administration building. "I'd like to show you something special," Mrs. Arias said with a twinkle in her eye.

She ushered Nancy into her office and opened a door at the back of the room. Nancy realized they were in the conference room she had been in when she, Bess, and George had come to the ranch earlier. At the far end, she saw the door that she knew led to Mr. Arias's office.

"Marco, could you come here, please?" Mrs. Arias called. Her husband walked into the room from his office. A slight chill danced down Nancy's spine as she remembered him striding toward her closet hiding space the day before. He was dressed in an outfit that matched his wife's.

Mrs. Arias introduced Nancy to her husband and asked him to tell her about the expansion plans. They walked to the scale model that Nancy had seen two days earlier. "This will be a paradise when this plan is realized," Mrs. Arias said. "A paradise."

Mr. Arias pointed out the areas Nancy had already seen on her tour. He seemed nice enough to Nancy, but there was something she didn't like about him. Perhaps his broad smile seemed too automatic to her. Perhaps he seemed a bit too eager to say what he thought Nancy wanted to hear. In any case, Nancy found him a little too slick for her taste. When he pointed out the new areas of development on the model of the ranch, Nancy saw that they stretched to the ocean bluffs.

"I didn't realize you had a beachfront area," Nancy said. "That's wonderful."

"We don't exactly have it yet," Mr. Arias said smoothly. "But we will soon. Before long, the present owner of the property will be begging us to take her land."

Nancy could barely believe her ears. She was relieved that the tour was over. Mrs. Arias escorted Nancy back to her car and said goodbye. Nancy could hardly wait to report to Didi. She made the short drive back in record time.

"Mrs. Myers," Nancy said breathlessly as she stepped inside the lodge kitchen. "Do you know where Didi is?"

"Hi, Nancy!" Didi's clear voice rang out as she stepped from the walk-in freezer.

"I've just had an interesting talk with the Ariases," Nancy said.

"Tell me what happened," Didi said. "Tell me everything."

Nancy related what she had learned from Mr. and Mrs. Arias. She decided not to tell Didi about the troubling financial records she had found in Didi's office earlier until she could speak with her privately.

"I knew it!" Didi said. "Well, that does it. I can't think about anything but the festival right now, but it'll be over Sunday. Then I'm going to talk to Sheriff Jacobs. I'm going to insist that he keep Marcos and Martina from bothering me or my guests anymore."

Didi pushed a damp curl from her forehead and began popping the frozen pies into the microwave to thaw them. "Bess and George are already at the campfire, Nancy," she said. "We'll be starting the hamburgers in a few minutes."

"Anything you want me to take down there?" Nancy offered.

"No, you're a guest," Didi said, with a warm smile. "And you're doing enough already. Now, go on and join the others."

Nancy headed through the small dark wooded area to the campfire site on the bluff overlooking the ocean.

The setting sun shone a bright orange, and the sea rippled with sparkling coral-pink reflections. Benches, blankets, chairs, and stools were scattered around the fire. The smell of burning wood and roasting chicken filled the cool air.

George and Bess had staked out a couple of blankets, and Nancy joined them.

"Ken and Jay are going to be a little late," Bess said. "And they're bringing a date for you," she added with a grin.

"Thanks," Nancy said, then repeated the tale of her afternoon with the Ariases.

"Looks like Didi was right," George said. "The Ariases definitely want Opa's beachfront."

As they talked, Sam Shaw, the maintenance man, walked up. "Excuse me, Miss Drew," he said. "Didi asked me to tell you that you have a phone call. She's transferring it to your cottage."

"That must be Dad," Nancy said. "Maybe he found out more for me. I'll be right back," she told her friends.

As Nancy started back to the cottage, she noticed that it was a lot darker in the woods now. The orange sun had finally dropped into the sea, and the moon was hidden by a passing cloud.

Nancy felt a ripple down her back as she picked her way along the path. She heard a rustling noise to her right and she stopped, holding her breath. After a moment, a rabbit hopped out of the woods in front of her and then disappeared in the dense underbrush.

Hold on, Nancy told herself with a sigh. No need to get jumpy over a cute little bunny.

With a nervous giggle, she continued along the dark path. It felt like a tunnel to Nancy, with its dense growth. The trees swung across the path above her, their branches tangled. She could see the dim light of the cottage porch light ahead. It was nearly as far as the length of a football field. She heard another noise in the woods. It sounded like a twig breaking.

She walked faster, eager to tell her father about what she had discovered in the Opa files and at the dude ranch.

With one long stride, a figure stepped out of the woods a few yards in front of her, filling the path and startling Nancy. The figure completely blocked off the light from the cottage, and Nancy could barely see. She felt goose bumps prickling along her arms. She couldn't tell who it was, but she did know that the person did not want her to pass.

Nancy's eyes widened as she tried to make out who it was. The large body was silhouetted as the cloud drifted past the moon.

Nancy felt a tight knot form in her stomach as she looked around quickly. If she turned and ran back to the campfire, she knew she'd be overtaken by the hulking form now blocking her way. Fighting a sense of rising panic, Nancy realized she was trapped.

8

The Case Is Solved?

"Who are you?" Nancy said. "I can't see your face. What do you want?"

"It's Barney Shaw," the man said. "And I want to talk to you."

"Barney!" Nancy said. She felt only slight relief when she realized it was Cal's stable hand. He was large like his brother, with a shadow of dark whiskers around his chin. Nancy felt uneasy about the menacing way in which he spoke.

Nancy stood firm, but she was ready to run if she needed to. "I can't talk now, Barney," she said.

"Well, I say we're going to talk right now," Barney said. "Just tell me what you know about Hubbard Wilson and then you can go take your call."

Nancy realized with a jolt of terror that she

hadn't mentioned her phone call to him. How did he know? Had she been set up for this ambush? she thought in a panic.

Nancy took another step forward, but Barney didn't move. "Look," she said. "Didi and Cal aren't going to be happy to hear that you're jumping out and bothering Opa guests. Let me by—right now!"

Barney started down the path toward her. His teeth were clenched, and his words came out in little spurts.

"I don't care about Opa or Didi or you," he said. "Now, you tell me what you found out or you're going to be real sorry."

"Okay, okay," Nancy said, thinking fast. She knew if she screamed that it would take a few minutes for anyone to find her. She might be able to outrun him back to the campfire, but she couldn't be sure. She decided to bluff her way out.

"We found a map," she said. "It was old and handmade and looked like a treasure map to some gold. We found it in the closet in a secret compartment in the floor. We gave it to Didi, and I think she turned it over to the sheriff."

At that moment the moon came out from behind a cloud, and Nancy could see Barney's face. His eyes were gleaming, and she could tell she'd hit the mark with her story. He seemed clearly excited by the news of the map.

"What did it say?" he asked. "Where's the gold?"

"We really didn't look at it very closely," Nancy said. "We'd just gotten here. We don't know any of the landmarks around Big Sur, so it didn't make much sense to us."

For a moment Barney's expression turned to anger, and Nancy was alarmed about what he might do. Then he gazed into the woods and muttered, "Sheriff Jacobs's got it, huh?"

He turned back to Nancy. "Forget that map and forget this meeting, do you hear me? If you tell anyone about what happened here, you and your friends can kiss your happy vacation goodbye."

Nancy nodded, and just as suddenly as he had appeared, Barney disappeared into the woods.

The encounter with Barney had been so quick that Nancy wondered for a moment if it had actually happened. Her trembling hands told her it had. She raced down the path to the main lodge.

Nancy burst into the kitchen and told Didi about her confrontation with Barney.

"There was no phone call for you," Didi said.

"Then I *was* set up," Nancy said. "And Barney's brother, Sam, was in on it, since he was the one who told me I had a phone call."

"Let's get Cal," Didi said. "He's down at the campfire. He'll help me fire those two."

Nancy quickly walked the path through the woods once more, this time with Didi and without any surprises. "I don't know too much about the Shaw brothers," Didi admitted as they

71

walked. "They had worked for Uncle Nick. He seemed to think they were okay, so I hired them."

Nancy thought of Didi's uncle and the words she overheard him say into the phone. She wondered whether the Shaw brothers could be on Nick's payroll.

Didi called Cal away from the campfire and quickly explained what had happened.

Cal joined them to search the area for Barney and Sam, but they couldn't find them. Didi called Sheriff Jacobs. He said he'd keep an eye out for them, especially since Nancy had told Barney that the sheriff had the map.

Didi also mentioned what Marco Arias had told Nancy about getting Didi to give up Opa soon. Sheriff Jacobs shook his head, saying that he wished Didi and the Ariases could just sit down and talk it out.

After Sheriff Jacobs and Cal left, Didi sank into a chair on the dining deck. "What am I going to do?" she said. "The biggest day of the year at Opa is tomorrow, and I'm short two people. Things are bad enough around here without my own employees deceiving me."

Didi frowned and her expression was dark and determined. "I know Marco was behind this, too," she said. "He probably paid the Shaw brothers to make trouble for me. What am I going to do? If he's trying to drive me crazy so I'll give in and sell Opa, I'm afraid it's working."

Didi's expression softened and she bit her lower lip. Nancy thought she looked like a scared little girl.

"I know some of it is my fault," Didi admitted. "I'm not the best business manager, I guess."

"Your parents must have thought you could do the job," Nancy said gently. "After all, they left Opa to you to run."

"With Uncle Nick's help," Didi said. "If he weren't managing the trust fund, I'd really be in a mess. Business has been so bad this past year, Opa would have gone under without him. He was able to work it out so that some of the trust fund money could be put into Opa to help support it. That was a big help." She smiled weakly at Nancy.

"It never seems to be enough, though," Didi continued. "There are so many improvements I'd like to make, but there's just not enough money. Maybe Uncle Nick's right. Maybe I'm just too young to handle this place."

"Who does he think should be in charge?" Nancy asked.

"He's never said," Didi answered. "He misses my mom a lot, I know. He probably just means that it would be great if Mom and Dad were still alive and taking care of things like always."

"Have you ever thought that he might mean himself?" Nancy asked gently. "Maybe he believes that the property would be better off if he took it over."

"What do you mean?" Didi said, giving Nancy a surprised look. "Are you saying he thinks he should have gotten Opa instead of me—because my mom was his sister?"

"I just meant that—" Nancy began.

"I can see where you're going with this, Nancy," Didi said. "And you're wrong. I'm sure of it. Uncle Nick is practically the only person in the world I can trust anymore."

"I'm sorry, Didi," Nancy said quickly. "I didn't mean to hurt your feelings, but—"

"Forget it," Didi said with a sigh. "I know you're trying to help. I'd better go help serve the ice cream—if there's anything left of it this late."

Nancy and Didi took a golf cart back to the campfire. Nearly everyone had gone. Cal and Mrs. Myers were packing up the leftover food. Nancy took Bess and George aside to fill them in on what had happened. Then Ken and Jay talked Bess and George into a moonlight walk along the bluff.

Nancy helped Mrs. Myers and Didi clean up, then headed back for the cottage. After a shower, she changed to her sleepshirt. Then she built a little fire in the fireplace and settled in front of it to think through the case.

Was Marco Arias behind the sabotage at Opa? He certainly was talking as if he knew that the lodge was going under soon. And he certainly seemed eager to cash in on it. He had brought up some of the legal issues Didi had to fight—

zoning, for instance—but there was no proof that he was involved in any of the illegal incidents.

Nancy next considered the Shaw brothers. They probably were the ones who'd torn Hubbard Wilson's cottage apart to find clues about the miner's gold stash, she concluded, but what about the other incidents at Opa? Were they responsible for those, too?

If they had found out that Nancy and her friends were looking into the problems at Opa, they might have cut Bess's saddle and the television cable to discourage the investigation.

Nancy couldn't figure out why the Shaw brothers would try to ruin Opa and Didi. They had no reason to—at least that she knew about.

Nick Prenopoulos's involvement in any kind of scheme was still just a hunch, Nancy had to remind herself. There was some money unaccounted for, it was true, but Didi was a poor manager by her own admission. Maybe the records were just wrong. If money was embezzled, did Didi's uncle Nick take it? Did Didi know and was she covering for him? But then, if Didi did know, Nancy thought, why was she so eager to have Nancy take on the case?

Could Didi have taken the money from the trust herself for some reason? Nancy laughed to herself as she thought about how farfetched her theories were getting. Time for a good night's sleep, she thought as she stood up and stretched.

Nancy's musings were interrupted by the phone. It was Didi.

"I've got really big news, Nancy," Didi said. "But first, I want to say something. I'm sorry I got upset with you earlier."

"Hey, no problem," Nancy assured her.

"It's just that so much has happened lately, I'm pretty spooked," Didi said. "I asked you to help me figure out what's been going on around here. I knew you had to check everything. No one's above suspicion, right? Not even Uncle Nick."

"Right," Nancy said.

"Well, you don't have to worry about it anymore," Didi said. "Here's my big news. The case is solved!"

9

Nancy Accused

"Solved?" Nancy said in disbelief. "When did this happen?"

"Sheriff Jacobs just called," Didi said. "Sam and Barney have been picked up and charged. It's over, Nancy. The nightmare at Opa is over!"

"That's wonderful, Didi," Nancy said. "What are the Shaws charged with?"

"The Shaws?" George said, bursting into the cottage. "Sam and Barney? I'm glad they were found."

Bess followed her cousin in and closed the door. She yawned loudly as she sank onto the footstool in front of the fire. Nancy signaled for quiet so she could hear Didi over the phone.

"They were charged with breaking and entering and destruction of property so far," Nancy heard Didi say, answering Nancy's question. "But there'll be more."

Nancy covered the receiver and quickly repeated to Bess and George what Didi had told her, then asked Didi, "Were they looking for Hubbard Wilson's gold?"

"Yes," Didi answered. "Their grandfather had been one of Hubbard's mining buddies. They grew up hearing the legend about the prehistoric cave in Pico Cielo. The only reason they came to work here was because they knew the old cottage had been built by Hubbard. They figured it might have a map or some clue in it about Hubbard's gold strike."

"How did the sheriff know for sure that they were the ones who did the damage?" Nancy asked. "Did they confess?"

"Sheriff Jacobs got a tip," Didi said. "Someone in the village overheard them bragging about how easy it had been to break into the cottage. They said they were determined to find Hubbard's gold. When they were arrested, Sam told Sheriff Jacobs that they hadn't meant to tear the place up, but they got mad when they didn't find anything. As Barney said, they went a little nuts."

"They sure did," Nancy agreed. "And for nothing."

"Oh, I almost forgot," Didi said. "Barney cut Bess's saddle strap. He thought you three were snooping around and getting too close, so he tried to discourage you."

"Well, it didn't work," Nancy said. "That must

be why they ambushed me in the woods. Did Sheriff Jacobs ask them about the television cable that fell into the pool?"

"Yes, he did," Didi answered. "But they said they don't know anything about that. Cal's probably right. Some animal must have bitten through it."

Nancy thanked Didi for her call, then hung up. She repeated the last part of the conversation to Bess and George.

"Well, I'm glad that's over," Bess said, yawning as she walked back to the bedroom. "Now maybe we can have a real vacation."

"Maybe," Nancy said. "I'm not so sure."

George followed Bess to the bedroom and Nancy climbed the ladder to her sleeping loft. In spite of her lingering doubts, she was asleep in minutes.

Saturday was bright and clear—a perfect day for the outdoor festival, Nancy thought as she looked at the picture-perfect view from the living room window. The ocean looked calm and peaceful. She set out juice and rolls for a light breakfast.

"I'm still full from the campfire supper," George said as she emerged from the bedroom a short while later. "And today's the Greek Festival," she added with a groan. "I'll have to double my workouts when we get home."

"Speaking of last night, how was the moonlight walk?" Nancy said, her eyes twinkling. "And what happened to the guy they were bringing for me?"

"Wonderful," Bess said, her expression dreamy. "Ken said he might even come to River Heights for Thanksgiving. Wouldn't that be wonderful?"

"My walk was okay, too," George said. "Jay's pretty cool. Actually, your guy is a volunteer firefighter," she said to Nancy. "He was on a run last night. He's coming to the festival today."

"I'll believe he exists when I see him." Nancy laughed.

"Well, at least you're back on vacation," Bess said. "The case is solved."

"Do you think it is, Nancy?" George asked.

"I'm not so sure," Nancy answered. Her eyebrows were pulled together as she frowned in concentration.

"I knew it," Bess said. "George and I were talking about it before we went to sleep last night. We could tell you didn't think the Shaw brothers were behind everything."

"I just want to make sure, that's all," Nancy said. "I thought a lot about it last night before you two came home. For example, what about the television cable? I was sure someone was watching us when we walked up to the pool. Was it really just a coincidence that the cable broke— or was chewed through—at the moment that George was diving in?"

"But if it wasn't an accident, it was probably cut by Sam or Barney, right?" George said.

"Yeah," Bess agreed. "It was another warning to us to get off the case, to stop looking into the problems here at Opa."

"Then why didn't they confess to that, too?" Nancy said. "They confessed to everything else, but not that. No one was hurt—it was just a broken cable. Why not admit to that if they admitted to everything else?"

Bess and George were quiet while they thought over Nancy's words. Nancy looked out the window at the bright ocean, sparkling with sunlight. "I want to learn more about Hubbard Wilson and his cabinetmaking skills," she said finally. "I'm glad we're going to Cloud Palace tomorrow. Maybe we'll get to see some of his handiwork and find out more about his mining treasures."

"I just want to see the estate," Bess said. "If it looks like the brochure, it's amazing."

From a distance, they could hear the Greek band tuning up for the festival. "Let's get ready to party!" George said as she pushed her chair back and did a few dance steps.

They quickly finished their juice and rolls and washed the breakfast dishes. Then they took turns in the shower and began getting ready for the festival.

Bess wore a blue flowered dress that perfectly matched her eyes. George chose her white jeans and a cropped white T-shirt. Nancy dressed last, in turquoise shorts and matching shirt.

"Hi, girls!" Didi greeted them as they approached the clearing. A broad smile stretched across her pretty face. She was wearing a long green skirt topped with a flowered vest in blue and green. Under the vest she had on a pale blue sheer blouse with long flowing sleeves gathered at the cuffs. Nancy thought she had perfectly captured the colors of the Big Sur sky and ocean.

"Isn't it a beautiful day?" Didi said. "I couldn't ask for better weather if I'd ordered it."

"It's great," Bess agreed.

"Today is going to be especially sweet now that Sam and Barney are behind bars," Didi continued. "All this time I was so sure it was Marco Arias causing the trouble around here by himself. Now I find out my own employees are in on his scheme."

"Don't be too hard on yourself, Didi," George said. "We've all been fooled at one time or another."

Didi's expression brightened. "Well, the main thing is that the Shaws have been caught and can't do any more harm. And Marco won't be far behind. Once they confess that he hired them, it's over."

"Are you saying that you believe Mr. Arias hired the Shaws to create problems at Opa?" Nancy asked. "But I thought the Shaws were after the gold and that's why they vandalized the cottage."

"Oh, sure," Didi said with a nod. "But that doesn't let Marco off the hook. You yourself heard Marco talking about his plan for his resort.

He's determined to get Opa. What better way than to hire my own employees to sabotage me? Sheriff Jacobs will get the whole truth out of them eventually."

"I sure hope so," Nancy said.

"Well, have fun," Didi said as she turned to go back to the main lodge. "See you later."

"She's sure not going to let Mr. Arias off the hook, is she?" Bess said.

"I guess not," Nancy said.

"Can we just put the case out of our minds for a few hours?" George said. "I hear music—I've just got to dance!"

"You win," Nancy said. "Let's go."

Nancy and her friends walked on toward the clearing. Didi and her staff had turned Opa into an outdoor Greek fair and marketplace. People young and old were wandering around, clearly enjoying the food, music, and dancing.

At the edge of the clearing, booths had been set up, arched with the flowers and vines that Nancy and her friends had gathered.

The three wandered from booth to booth. Vendors sold T-shirts, handmade jewelry, leather goods, baskets, and carved wood items.

Under Mrs. Myers's supervision, local villagers sold homemade Greek pastries, honey puffs, sandwiches, and soft drinks from four booths.

Growers from the area offered free samples of olives and almonds from their groves. Down by the campfire circle, lamb roasts turned on spits.

After an hour and a half of wandering around,

the aromas of all the food were irresistible. "I'm famished," Bess said. "I'm going to get some lunch."

"Me, too," George said. "Let's get some sandwiches."

Shouts of "O-pa" drew Nancy's attention to a booth with a line of waiting customers. "I wonder what's going on there," she said. "I'm going to check it out. I'll catch up with you later."

George and Bess got in line at the sandwich booth, while Nancy joined the crowd at the booth with the word *Saganaki* written above it. Three men in embroidered shirts and fishermen's caps were busy behind the counter filling orders.

"What is saganaki?" Nancy asked a young woman standing nearby.

"It means flaming cheese," the woman said. "Watch."

One of the men behind the counter put a six-inch square of cheese on a grill. Nancy could smell the toasty fragrance as it sizzled. When it began to melt, he scraped it up and put it on a plate.

The second man poured a little brandy on it. Then, with a grand flourish, he lit it with a match. As it burst into two-foot-high flames, the crowd yelled "O-pa."

The cheese flamed until Nancy knew every drop of alcohol had burned off. Then the third man squeezed a wedge of lemon over it to douse the flames. The cheese, now melted inside but with a crunchy, lemony crust, was ready to serve.

Nancy couldn't resist the show and the aroma, and she bought one.

Nancy, Bess, and George took their sandwiches and sodas to a picnic table to eat. A Greek band played nearby. The canyons were filled with the sounds of laughter mixed with the melodic folk music. Small children, preteens, and teenagers, all in brightly colored costumes, joined long lines of dancers across and around the clearing.

As Nancy and her friends finished their meal, Mrs. Myers hurried up to their table. She seemed a little frazzled. "I hate to ask you, but I need your help," she said.

"Of course, Mrs Myers," Nancy said. "What can we do?"

"A friend of mine and her daughter were running the honey puffs booth. They've been called home for an emergency," Mrs. Myers said. "I've found replacements for them, but they won't be here for half an hour. Didi hated to ask you, but she's really desperate for help. She will pay you, of course."

Nancy looked at the others, who each nodded. "We'd be happy to, Mrs. Myers," she said. "It would be fun. And we certainly won't take any money for it. Just consider it our contribution to the restoration of Opa."

"Hannah was right," Mrs. Myers said as she gave Nancy a quick hug. "You are an angel." She led them back to the booth and showed them the procedure.

"The honey puffs are already cooked." Mrs. Myers indicated a huge container brimming with what looked like little golden pillows of dough.

"When you get an order, fill one of these paper boats," she continued. "It should take about five puffs. Sprinkle them with powdered sugar and cinnamon. Then drizzle honey over the whole order."

Mrs. Myers scurried away, leaving Nancy, Bess, and George to fill the orders for the long line that was forming in front of the booth.

"This is fun," Bess said, drizzling honey over an order. "I love the music. As soon as Ken gets here, we're going to the clearing. I'm going to dance the rest of the day."

"I'm going to *have* to dance," Nancy said. "Just to work off all the honey puffs I keep popping in my mouth while we—"

"There they are," a voice boomed through the crowd, interrupting Nancy. "There—in that booth. Those three young women."

Nancy's face flushed red as Marco Arias stormed toward their booth. He pushed through the line and pointed right at her. "Arrest all three of them," Mr. Arias said. "Arrest them now!"

10

Terror at the Festival

"What are you waiting for?" Mr. Arias said to Sheriff Jacobs. "I insist you arrest these girls now."

Marco Arias and the sheriff stood in front of the counter. Nancy heard Bess gasp. Mr. Arias wheeled to point at Bess and George.

"They were the first," he yelled. "They prowled around my ranch, passing themselves off as would-be guests. They got my secretary all worked up over some story about puppies," he blustered.

He looked back at Nancy. "And this one came to the ranch and passed herself off to me and my wife as a potential client," he said. "Now I see they are all working for Opa! I'm sure that Didi Koulakis hired them to spy on me. That's corporate espionage."

Nancy saw Didi making her way through the gathering crowd. Even from a distance, Nancy could see tears glinting in the young woman's eyes.

"Please," Didi pleaded. "Can we do this privately? There's no need to upset the festival-goers. Let's go to my office. We can settle things there."

Sheriff Jacobs nodded, and he and Didi started toward the main lodge, followed by Mr. Arias. Mrs. Myers arrived with the helpers for the honey puffs booth. Nancy and her friends were relieved of their duties and hurried quickly to follow the others.

They finally reached the privacy of Didi's office. Didi crumpled in the chair behind her desk. "Didi," Sheriff Jacobs said sternly, "do you want to tell me what's going on?"

Didi seemed unable to talk. She looked at Nancy, her eyes still full of tears.

"Sheriff," Nancy said. "My friends and I are not employees of Opa. You know yourself that we were staying in the Hubbard cabin when it was ransacked. We're guests at Opa. We were simply helping out for a while because of a family emergency regarding one of the vendors."

"I don't believe it," Mr. Arias snorted.

"It is true," Didi said. She stood and Nancy could tell she had regained her composure. "You really have a nerve," Didi said to Mr. Arias.

Didi turned to Sheriff Jacobs. "I have contacted you several times over the past year about problems we have had here. I was sure Mr. Arias had something to do with them. And now he's trying to wreck my festival. Arrest *him!*"

Didi and Mr. Arias exchanged angry looks.

"Now, look, you two," Sheriff Jacobs began. "There are a lot of wild charges being flung around here. If either of you wants to come to my office and fill out papers filing formal charges, do it."

Mr. Arias seemed to calm down a little, and Didi took a small step back.

"I can tell you that nothing is going to be done tonight," Jacobs continued. "I suggest we all relax and enjoy the fun and festivities."

"Not him," Didi said. "I want him off Opa."

"No," Mr. Arias said simply. "I've done nothing wrong. I'm staying. I want to make sure everyone knows what's going on."

"Are you sure that's all you want to do, Mr. Arias?" Nancy asked. "You can't fulfill your plans for expansion unless you own Opa. Perhaps you're here checking out Didi's operation so you can move in on it. Perhaps you're doing a little corporate spying yourself."

"Okay," Jacobs said, standing up. "Here's the way it's going to be. You three," he said, pointing to Nancy, Bess, and George, "stay away from the Arias Dude Ranch. Didi, I want you to stop your accusations. And you," he said, putting his hand on Marco Arias's shoulder, "stay away from Opa."

"That means leaving now," Didi said.

"That's right," Sheriff Jacobs agreed, guiding Mr. Arias to the door. "I want you all to stick to this plan," he said without turning around.

After the men had left, Didi crumpled in her chair again. "Well, that's it. The festival is ruined. All that commotion . . . the sheriff coming . . . the crowd gathering. It's a disaster."

"I don't know," Nancy said, looking out Didi's office window. "It looks pretty lively out there."

The others joined Nancy at the window. The sun had set and the twilight glow showed a throng of people dancing, eating, and apparently having a wonderful time.

"I don't know about you guys," Bess said, "but I'm going to find Ken and go dancing."

She and George left for the clearing. Didi put her arm around Nancy's shoulders. "I can't thank you enough, Nancy," she said. "I was so upset earlier, I couldn't talk. This festival is so important. It's a huge moneymaker, and we count on its success."

For a moment Nancy considered telling Didi about her uncle's phone conversation that she had overheard. But realizing that it would only upset Didi further, she decided to wait until after the festival, when things calmed down a bit.

"Well, it looks like it's going to be fine after all," Nancy said. "Put Mr. Arias out of your mind. You heard the sheriff. He can't come back here, so enjoy the rest of the festivities."

"You know, I think I will," Didi said with a grin. "Let's go!"

Nancy and Didi left the main lodge to return to the festival. Didi went directly to the honey puffs booth to check on the new people working there.

Nancy wandered over to a small area in the cedar grove that had been set aside for a Greek coffeehouse. Small tables and benches were scattered around the area, and men served Greek coffee, cinnamon tea, and tiny sugared sesame biscuits.

Nancy sat on one of the benches and ordered a cup of tea. After a few minutes, she was joined by two women whom she judged to be in their thirties.

"Hi," one of them said, smiling. "My name is Melissa. This is Pam. We come to this festival every year."

"This is my first time," Nancy said. "My friends and I are here on vacation."

"Isn't it fun?" Melissa said. "It's especially great to come and relax after a hard week at work."

"What do you do?" Nancy asked.

"We're California park rangers," Pam said. "We're guides at Cloud Palace down the coast."

"We're going there tomorrow," Nancy said.

"That's great," Melissa said. "We're both off duty tomorrow, but our friend Kristi will be working. You'll have a great tour."

"When was the place built?" Nancy asked, hoping to get some information that would tie in to Hubbard Wilson.

"The construction began in 1900," Pam said.

"And it took the rest of Mr. Cloud's life to build. In fact, it never was really completed. He was still adding things when he died."

"I've heard about a wood carver who worked on the construction there for three years," Nancy said. "His name was Hubbard Wilson."

The two women looked at each other, then finally shook their heads.

"I've never heard of him," Melissa said. "But if he was there then, he probably worked on one of the guest bungalows. They were built first."

Pam laughed. "Wait till you see them," she said. "They call them bungalows, but they're elegant mansions."

"I'm really looking forward to tomorrow's trip," Nancy said. "About how long does it take to get there?"

"A little over an hour," Pam answered. "It's not that far, but the coast road is narrow and winding, so drive carefully."

"Well, I'm refreshed," Melissa said. "It's time to check out the T-shirts."

The two rangers left with a friendly wave goodbye. Nancy finished her tea and decided to find Bess and George. She wandered down to the clearing where the band was playing.

Bess, Ken, George, and Jay were dancing in a long line that snaked around another line of dancers. A girl in Greek costume, who appeared to Nancy to be about ten years old, was leading Bess and George's line. She wore a long cherry red skirt, a white blouse, and a pink vest criss-crossed with black laces.

The girl held a white handkerchief high in her right hand. Her left hand held Bess's right hand. Bess, in turn, held Ken's hand, and on it went down the long line.

"Come on, Nancy," George called. "Join us." She and Jay broke hands and Nancy jumped in to fill the gap. Following the footsteps of the people in front of her, Nancy settled into the dance. Step right, hop, step left, hop, step back, cross over, repeat.

The music gradually got faster, then even faster. Everyone laughed and cheered as they mastered the steps. The line moved like a rattle-snake, in several short waves. Nancy began to feel a little dizzy as they twisted and turned.

Suddenly, she heard a strange whoosh from the area where the food vendors were located. Then—*ka-boom!*—a horrifying explosion tore through the air, followed closely by a woman's scream.

11

Run, Nancy!

"Call the fire squad!" someone yelled. "And an ambulance! Where's Sheriff Jacobs?" someone else cried. "I saw him a little while ago."

The band stopped playing, and several members laid down their instruments, jumped from the little stage, and ran toward the food area.

The dancers stumbled to a stop. Nancy, Bess, George, and their friends followed the others running to help.

Flames bounced from one booth to another around the ring. Didi, Cal, and one of the security guards hired for the day aimed hoses at the fire. Others formed a bucket brigade from the stream. Even with this effort, the fire seemed especially stubborn. Just when the flames seemed to be snuffed out, they flared up again.

People—some injured, some in shock—sat on

the ground or leaned against trees. Mrs. Myers and others offered them sips of water.

Nancy, Bess, and George helped rescuers herd people away from the fire. They urged those that had been injured to remain where they were. They asked people who seemed all right to either help or keep a safe distance.

"What happened?" Nancy asked Mrs. Myers as they helped a woman to a chair.

"I don't know," Mrs. Myers said, her voice trembling. "I think it started in the saganaki booth. I was helping fill orders for honey puffs, and I heard an explosion. I just don't know."

The paramedics arrived and went right to work. Nancy and George joined Jay, Bess, and Ken in the water brigade, and they were soon assisted by the volunteer fire squad with its truck and hose. Finally, the flames were extinguished.

Nancy found Didi, who was standing with two firefighters. "Didi, what happened?" she asked. "Have there been any serious injuries?"

"The saganaki booth blew up," Didi said. She sounded exhausted and defeated. "Fortunately, most of the guests were dancing and away from the area."

Didi wiped her sooty face with the ruined sleeve of her blouse. "Two of the men in the saganaki booth were injured, but they're going to be okay. The paramedics are rushing them to the hospital."

Nancy remembered the laughing men who had

prepared her flaming cheese. "I'm so happy to hear they'll be okay," she said.

"Some people suffered cuts and bruises, mainly from running or being dragged away from danger," Didi continued. "They got first aid, and they'll be okay, too. The paramedics took the ones close to the explosion to the hospital to check for hearing damage. Some are being treated for smoke inhalation."

"Do they know what caused the explosion?" Nancy asked.

"The fire marshal told me it looked as if a powerful explosive had been added to the brandy they pour over the cheese. When one of the men lit it, it knocked him clear out the back of the booth. That's what saved him from being burned more seriously."

"Do you mean it was arson?" Nancy asked.

"Of course," Didi said. "It wasn't an accident, Nancy. Marco Arias is so determined to get this place, he'll do anything—even have someone try to blow up the place." She brushed back her thick brown hair with her hand. "Well, he's won. I'm glad I have some reserve money. It will probably take all of my trust fund to pay for the damages."

Didi walked off slowly, her shoulders slumped.

Bess and George ran up. "What a mess," George said. "Did you find out what happened?"

Nancy repeated what Didi had told her.

"It takes an awful person to do something like this," Bess said.

"I need a shower," George said. "There really isn't anything more we can do now. Sheriff Jacobs won't allow any cleaning up until they've gone over everything for evidence. You coming, Nancy?"

"You two go ahead," Nancy said. "I still have to tell Didi what I've found out about her uncle Nick and her money."

"Now?" Bess asked. "Oh, Nancy, do you have to? She's so upset about the explosion and everything."

"I was going to wait," Nancy said. "I don't want to add to her problems, but I can't delay any longer. I'm sure the fire marshal is going to look into this. If he finds reason to suspect arson, there will be more investigation. If Didi's uncle is involved, she needs to be prepared."

"Poor Didi," Bess said. "What a mess."

"I'll be at the cottage later," Nancy said. She watched her friends start down the cedar-lined path. Then she turned back toward the main lodge.

Her heart sank when she saw Didi in her office. Her beautiful outfit was blotched with soot and stained from the fire extinguishing foam. She sat in her desk chair, looking out the window.

"Didi," Nancy said gently. "I have to talk to you." She stepped inside and closed the door.

"Well, he got me again," Didi said, shaking her head slowly.

"Who do you mean?" Nancy asked.

"Marco, of course," Didi said. "Who else could have done it? Sam and Barney didn't cause the explosion. They're locked up."

Didi stood up and began pacing. "As soon as I relaxed," she continued, "when I was sure that Sheriff Jacobs was finally taking charge, Marco pulls his worst stunt. I don't know how I'm going to recover from this one, Nancy. The Greek Festival helps us get through some of the leaner months. But this year . . ." She returned to her desk and took a sip from her teacup.

"Would you like some tea?" Didi asked. "Herbal tea helps me feel better. This is apple ginger."

"Thanks," Nancy said. "That sounds good."

Didi went to the small table under the window and poured Nancy a cup of steaming tea from a thermal pitcher. When Nancy took the cup, the fragrance of spicy fruit filled the air.

"You said you wanted to talk to me," Didi said, sitting back down. "I suppose you girls have decided to check out early. You won't be the only ones, I'm sure. The fire marshal and sheriff agreed they need to look into what happened today."

"No, no, that's not it," Nancy said. "We're not leaving. But it is about the investigation and what might turn up."

"What do you mean?" Didi said, leaning forward. "Have you discovered something?"

"It's not about Marco Arias," Nancy said softly. "It's about your uncle."

"Uncle Nick? What about him?" Didi took another sip of tea.

Nancy told her about the trust records, then sat quietly while Didi absorbed the news.

"We've had some pretty bad times around here," Didi said finally. "I'm not surprised he dipped into the trust fund. But I'm sure it was used for Opa bills, in spite of what the records show. Look, Nancy, Uncle Nick wouldn't do anything to hurt me or Opa."

Nancy wasn't sure that Didi understood the full implication of what Nancy had told her. "Didi, I overheard your uncle on the phone Thursday after our meeting about the Greek Festival," she said gently. "Someone apparently was demanding money. He said that the person would be getting it soon, and that Opa should have been his. He said it would be—no matter what it takes."

"Are you saying he might be behind the sabotage so that he can get Opa?" Didi asked, her face suddenly pale. "You have to be mistaken. Why would Uncle Nick take money from Opa? From me?"

"My dad's an attorney, just like your uncle," Nancy said. "I asked him to check around." Nancy put her cup down on the corner of Didi's desk. "Did you know Nick has quite a reputation as a gambler?"

"Sure, I know about it," Didi said. "He likes to go to the races and to Las Vegas." She looked intently at Nancy as the full weight of the accusation reached her. "You think he's embezzled money from the trust fund to pay off his gambling debts?" she said with a gasp.

"Perhaps," Nancy said. "Be prepared. If an investigation is launched, all this may come out."

"Come on," Didi said. "Let's settle this right now. I'm sure he's still here."

"Wouldn't you like to talk to him alone?" Nancy asked.

"No. I'd like you to come with me," Didi said. "If you're right, I'm going to need a friend."

They found Didi's uncle sitting alone on the dining deck. They joined him at the small table. Without any lead-in at all, Didi blurted out what Nancy had told her about the missing funds.

"What!" her uncle said. He seemed stunned, then flustered. "I don't know what you . . . I audit those records myself," he sputtered. "There's nothing wrong there . . . how could you . . ." He stopped talking and looked around quickly. For a moment, Nancy thought he was going to run away.

"Uncle Nick," Didi said gently, "Nancy heard you talking to someone on the phone about money. And I know you've racked up some gambling debts. Please be honest with me."

Nick Prenopoulos pulled his shoulders up, and his dark eyes darted from Didi to Nancy and back to Didi. Nancy thought he was going to begin blustering again, but suddenly he crumpled. He looked down at the table. His hands began twisting a blue-striped napkin.

"Uncle Nick," Didi said firmly. "Why aren't you defending yourself? How could you do it?"

"I only borrowed the money," he said. "I'd done it before and always put it back. It was a loan. I'd never do anything to hurt you," he said, sitting down and putting his head in his hands.

"I know that, Uncle Nick, but you need help," Didi said. "Gambling is a serious problem."

"I know that," he said, nodding. "I knew it would all come out eventually. I'm sorry. I'll get help, I promise. There's a place in Carmel that helps people with gambling problems. I'll go up tomorrow and see someone there."

"What about the sabotage around here?" Nancy asked. "Did you have anything to do with it?"

"Be honest, Uncle Nick," Didi said. "Nancy overheard you say that Opa should have been yours and would be, no matter what. Did you cause some of the problems around here so I'd pull out and you could take over—and maybe sell it to Arias? Have you been working with him to sabotage Opa?"

"No!" Nick Prenopoulos said, startled. "When I said Opa would be mine, I meant that you were getting so discouraged, I thought you might be close to giving it up. If so, I planned to buy it from you. Sure, I probably would have sold it to raise cash to pay off my debts—maybe even to Marco. But I would never have done anything to damage the property or endanger you or anyone else."

Didi looked at her uncle intently. "I believe

101

you," she said finally. "But you have to get help, Uncle Nick. I'll drive you to the clinic myself." She reached out and put her hand on his arm.

"I never meant to betray you," he said, shaking his head. "Wait a minute," he added. "I thought you said the Shaw brothers were responsible for everything that happened around here."

"But what about the explosion today?" Nancy said. "If it wasn't an accident, they sure didn't do it—unless, of course, they have an accomplice."

Nancy pushed her chair away from the table and stood. "Well, I'm sure you two have a lot to talk about, so I'll go back to the cottage. We want an early start tomorrow. We're going to Cloud Palace."

"You'll love it," Didi said, clearly trying to be enthusiastic, but she was obviously heartbroken. Nancy felt sorry for her new friend. Nick Prenopoulos was Didi's only relative and Nancy knew his embezzling—even if he planned to return the money—was hard for Didi to take.

As she walked back to the cabin, Nancy's thoughts were racing. Were the Shaw brothers and Nick all telling everything? If so, were the other incidents—the ones no one would confess to—accidents or not? Was there someone else Didi had to fear?

Nancy decided to talk with Cal about the report on the severed television cable and changed her course.

The sun had set. The security light cast an eerie glow over the burned-out festival booths.

Nancy saw Cal standing outside the stable. His back was to her and one arm was sweeping through the air with a broad gesture. He was talking to someone, but Nancy couldn't see who because his body blocked her view.

As she drew closer, Nancy heard Cal's voice. His voice was raised, and although she couldn't make out what he was saying, she could tell he was very angry. Occasionally, she heard the other man's voice, but she didn't recognize it.

Nancy ducked behind a tree and strained to hear the words, but she was too far away. She darted forward across the path to the shadows of a trash shed. Her heart racing, she crouched down behind the shed. Who was the man arguing with Cal and what were they talking about, she wondered. Why was Cal so furious?

As she moved behind the shed, she tripped over a large empty can. She caught herself, but the can rolled onto the path with a hollow clatter.

"Hey," the stranger yelled. "Who's there?"

Nancy held her breath as she moved her head just enough to peek out from behind the shed. She watched in horror as the man raced toward her.

"I see you, you little snoop," he yelled. "Get out of there—or I'll drag you out."

12

The Clue in the Castle

"Come on out," the stranger yelled as Nancy crouched behind the shed. "I know you're there."

She could hear footsteps pounding closer. She looked around frantically. There was no place to hide. She took a deep breath and stepped out onto the path.

The stranger approached her, his expression menacing. He was stocky, with a thick red beard. Cal ran up behind him and grabbed his shoulder. He wheeled the stranger around. "You're trespassing," Cal said. "I told you to leave Opa and I mean it."

The trespasser set his shoulders, and Nancy thought he was going to take a swing at Cal. Then he stomped off to a van parked beside the stable.

"Don't let me ever see you around here again,"

Cal called as the man sped away in a cloud of dust.

"Are you all right?" Cal asked Nancy, rushing to her side. "I hope he didn't scare you too much."

"No," Nancy answered. "I'm okay. Thanks for coming to my rescue. Who was he? What did he want?"

"He's one of the local men we hired to help with the festival," Cal answered. "He thought he should have been paid more. That's the last time we hire him. I doubt that he'll come back. If he does, a call to the sheriff should discourage him."

Cal picked up the can Nancy had kicked and dropped it into the Dumpster. "How come you were down here?" he asked Nancy.

"I wanted to ask you about the electrical technician's report," she answered.

"On the cable?" Cal said. "I found the squirrel that did it. He's tasted his last cable. It's not the first time that's happened around here," he said. "It's the price we pay for sharing the land with wild animals. I'm just happy you kept your friend out of the water before the cable hit."

"Me, too," Nancy said. She shuddered when she remembered the sizzle that shot through the pool. "Well, I guess I'll get back to the cottage."

Cal smiled, then turned and loped off toward his room above the stable.

Nancy hurried up the path and through the cedar grove to her cottage. George and Bess were already in their sleepshirts. Nancy changed quickly, then told them about her conversation with Didi and her uncle. She concluded with a breathless account of her adventure near the stable.

"Boy, I'm really looking forward to tomorrow," Bess said as the three headed for their beds.

"It'll be nice to get away," George agreed.

"I hate to say it," Nancy called down from the sleeping loft, "but I agree with you. Tomorrow we go to a completely different world—a real palace."

"A nice, safe place," Bess said sleepily, "where people live happily ever after."

Sunday morning was cloudy and cool. After coffee in their cabin, Nancy and her friends decided to skip breakfast at the lodge in favor of a quick bite on the road. Dressed in jeans and sweaters, they headed for the Mustang.

As Pam had told Nancy, the drive from Opa to Cloud Palace took a little over an hour.

"Oooh, there it is," Bess cried, when the legendary pink tower came into view. "That must be it."

Nancy saw Cloud Palace perched atop a small mountain in the near distance. She steered the car down a narrow winding road. At the foot of the mountain was a large parking lot.

"The brochure says to park the car in the lot and take a shuttle bus the rest of the way," George said from the backseat. "We've got an hour and ten minutes before our tour time. Let's eat. I'm starved."

Nancy drove past the tourist parking lot and on to the small coastal town of Seacove beyond. They had brunch at a small restaurant. "Let's leave the car here and walk back to the tourist area," Nancy suggested when they had finished eating. "We have time."

When they reached the parking lot, the guide, wearing a safari suit indicating she was a park ranger, was urging tourists aboard the shuttle van. She was a young brunette and appeared to be only a few years older than Nancy. She confirmed that she was Kristi, a friend of the two guides Nancy had met at the festival the night before.

Nancy, George, and Bess scrambled into the van and took seats in the back. Then the shuttle began the three-mile drive up the winding mountain road.

When they reached the top, their tour group organized outside the shuttle. "Before we start," Kristi said, "let me say a few words about security. You must stay with the group. Do not attempt to strike out on your own. If you do, you will be retrieved by one of our guard dogs."

Nancy glanced over to a huge oak tree. A guard in a ranger uniform held tightly to the leashes of two large dogs. All three looked eager for work.

As they began the tour, Nancy and her friends were astonished by what had been done to transform this remote area into a fairy-tale paradise.

"All the trees and flowers were brought up and planted," Kristi told them. "Everything had to be shipped into the tiny port at the bottom of the mountain and hauled up here, often by mules."

"Wow," George whispered. "No semis."

"You will see the three guest bungalows later," Kristi said. "They're mansions themselves. But first, let's take a look at the main palace."

The inside of the palace was as impressive as the outside. The mansion was more like a museum than a house, Nancy thought, with its valuable paintings and tapestries, pottery dating back to ancient Greece, rare volumes in the five thousand-book library. No expense had been spared, it seemed, to satisfy Alexander Cloud's wishes.

"I don't believe all the gold," Bess whispered to Nancy as they followed Kristi. "Real gold leaf is everywhere—on lamp shades, furniture. There's even gold in the paint on the doors!"

After a couple of hours, the group was herded into a reception area for light refreshments. Then the tour resumed in one of the guest houses.

Nancy stayed a pace or two behind the group. When they reached a small library, she gasped. "Look!" she whispered, pointing at the wall. There were built-in shelves on either side of the carved fireplace, and they had the same decorative border as the cupboard found in the Hubbard cottage at Opa. Branches and leaves trailed around, leading to a tree trunk in one corner. A fat bear climbed halfway up the trunk.

Nancy reached out to touch the bear's paw to see if it tripped a lever to a hidden compartment the way the one at Opa did. "Excuse me," Kristi called out as Nancy reached toward the wall. "Please do not touch anything."

Blushing, Nancy pulled her hand back. Everyone in the group was staring at her. She mumbled an apology and stepped back into the circle of tourists. Bess and George followed.

After the tour of two of the guest bungalows, the group was ushered into a gift shop and snack bar. "I'll say goodbye now," Kristi said. "You'll have an hour's break. Then you join another group for the final part of the tour—the gardens and private zoo. Finally, you will be escorted back to the shuttles for your trip down to the parking lot."

"I've got to get back to that guest house and see if that bookcase by the fireplace has a secret compartment like the cupboard at Opa," Nancy told George and Bess. "It's the same design exactly. I'll bet Hubbard Wilson carved those panels."

"How can we get back there?" Bess asked. "You heard what Kristi said. We're not allowed to leave the group. There are rangers and dogs everywhere."

"I want us to hide out until the palace closes to tourists," Nancy said.

"Just where do we hide?" George asked.

"While we've been touring, I've studied the security check-in boxes," Nancy said. "Accord-

ing to the schedules posted on the boxes, someone clocks in at the pool every two hours
from eight-thirty A.M. to eight-thirty P.M." She
checked her watch. "It's five-fifteen. Our tour is
supposed to end about six-thirty. Then the place
closes."

"This is exciting," George said, her eyes sparkling. "What's our plan?"

"While we're walking around the grounds,
stick close to me. When the opportunity is right,
we'll duck into a hedge or behind some bushes.
Then shortly after six-thirty, we'll slip into the
pool house," Nancy said. "We can wait there
until eight or so—before the security ranger
makes his rounds. It will be dark then and we can
sneak out."

"Do you know when they check the guest
house where the carved wood paneling is?" Bess
asked, concern in her voice.

"Nine o'clock," Nancy answered. "We should
be able to find out what we want to know before
then."

"But won't they miss us if we disappear from
the tour group?" Bess asked.

"Kristi said that after our break here, we join
another group with a different guide—one who
doesn't know us," Nancy pointed out. "It will be
easier for us to disappear in a larger crowd."

"And the Mustang's not parked in the lot,"
George added. "That's a lucky break."

"Exactly," Nancy said. "There won't be a
suspicious car left after hours to give us away."

110

"Haven't you forgotten one thing, though?" Bess asked. "How do we get back down there?"

"It's only three miles," Nancy said. "And all downhill. We'll walk. I've got my flashlight in my bag. It won't be hard."

"I don't know. . . ." Bess said.

"You can go down with the shuttle if you want," George said, "and wait for us in town. I'm staying with Nancy."

"Okay, I'm in," Bess said, shrugging her shoulders. "If you two can do it, so can I."

"That's the spirit," Nancy said.

Nancy's plan worked perfectly—even better than she'd hoped. The tour ended at the outdoor pool. Nancy watched the pool house door. A ranger made his six-thirty check-in by pulling the lever of the time clock box next to the door.

As he left, Nancy led Bess and George from column to column until they were at the pool house door. Within seconds, they ducked inside.

It was dark. They held their breath, waiting to see if they were missed. Nancy put her ear to the door. After ten minutes, she heard the tour group move away. "They're leaving," she whispered.

"I think we did it," George said.

"We won't know for sure until seven, but I think you're right," Nancy agreed.

The three sat on the floor, leaning against the wall. The smell of chlorine filled Nancy's nose. "Just think," she whispered. "Hubbard worked on his own cottage and this fantasyland at the same time. That must have been weird."

"Well, I could sure be happy here," Bess said. In the dim light, Nancy saw her friend's face. Bess's eyes were closed, and she was smiling dreamily.

"I wouldn't want to live here," George said. "Sure it's gorgeous, but I'd be happier in our cottage in the woods."

After a while, Nancy checked her watch. It was a few minutes past seven. "Let's go," she said.

Nancy opened the door and peered outside. Huge security lights glowed through the fog. She stepped out onto the pool deck. Bess and George followed.

Nancy's arms tingled as she looked around. The creeping fog seemed to change the shapes and contours of everything. Distant mountains seemed to move. It looked as if the palace tower were floating in the air.

"Follow me," Nancy said, "and stay close."

She headed straight for the guest house with the carved bookcase. She tripped the lock with her nail file, and they slipped inside. Then she used her penlight beam to light the way to the carved bear that matched the one in the Opa cottage.

"I was right!" Nancy said softly. "There's a hiding place." She reached into the small niche behind a shelf and pulled out an envelope. Nancy aimed the penlight beam. "It's a letter from Hubbard," she whispered. "It was sent to someone named Joan Lynn."

The girls heard a noise behind them. Nancy flipped off the light and put the letter in her pocket. Following the wall, Nancy began edging slowly around in the direction of the door. She could feel George and Bess following quietly behind.

There was a soft whoosh across the room, as if the door had shut. Nancy stopped. The three stood absolutely still, but she knew they were not alone.

The door had been closed from the inside. In the darkness, Nancy could hear the faint rhythm of someone breathing across the room.

13

A Hint from Hubbard

Nancy, Bess, and George stood very still, barely breathing. They knew someone else was in the room with them.

Suddenly, the crystal chandelier clicked on. The light was so intense that Nancy could hardly see for a few seconds. As her vision returned, she saw a park ranger standing by the door.

She started to stammer an explanation. But as the man came closer, a chill of horror rippled across the back of her neck. His features were distorted by a stocking pulled down over his face. Although he was grotesquely disguised, she could see the menacing threat in his eyes.

"Come on," she cried to Bess and George. The three rushed toward the door, pushing the man down as they ran by.

Nancy, George, and Bess raced across the

courtyard. The front door of Cloud Palace was ajar so they darted inside. As Nancy tried to slam the door and lock it, she felt it heaving toward her.

"Go!" she cried out to her friends. "He's right behind us."

Yelling for help, Nancy led the others around the palace, up and down staircases, through hallways, and in and out of rooms.

A few security lights lit their way once in a while. But most of the time, they relied on Nancy's penlight. The disguised ranger's footfalls beat a steady, terrifying rhythm behind them.

Nancy, Bess, and George ran up one long, dark, winding staircase. At the top, hallways stretched away on both sides. Straight ahead was a shorter staircase leading down to another level of the mansion.

There was no light at the top of the staircase except the penlight beam. Nancy saw a long, low footstool in the left hall. She remembered the tour guide telling them it had been used by Mr. Cloud's housekeeper to reach the candles in the wall sconces.

Nancy grabbed the footstool and placed it on the landing in front of the top of the stairs. She could hear their pursuer coming up the winding staircase behind them.

"Move!" Nancy whispered to the girls. "And make a lot of noise."

The three stepped over the long footstool, then

stormed down the short staircase and ducked under it to hide. With the light of Nancy's penlight gone, the stair landing, with the footstool trap Nancy had laid, was totally dark.

They could hear the man racing up the rest of the winding staircase. Then the footsteps stopped for a minute. Nancy was sure the man was listening, trying to figure out which way they had gone.

She coughed on purpose to encourage him to come down the short staircase. First, she heard him take two steps. Then she heard the clatter as his feet got tangled up with the footstool.

Nancy and her friends heard a surprised "Whoomph" at the top of the stairs. Then the man tumbled down the short staircase, landing in a crumpled heap at the foot of the steps.

"What's going on?" she heard a woman call out from the room beyond.

"Who's in there?" another voice yelled.

Nancy stepped out from the hiding place under the stairs and called back. "We're in here. Someone's chasing us."

The disguised ranger groaned as he stood up. There was something familiar about him, Nancy thought, but she could not put her finger on what it was. With one last menacing expression aimed right at her, he limped over to a glass door leading outdoors, opened it, and disappeared.

The lights flipped on, and two real security guards marched into the room. They both reached back to clutch the handles of their holstered guns.

"All right, start talking," one guard barked. She was pretty, with short blond hair under her ranger hat. Nancy could tell she was furious at finding them there.

Nancy talked quickly, eager to assure the two rangers that she and her friends meant no harm to the palace.

"We missed the last shuttle bus down to the parking lot," she said. She knew that was technically the truth—she just had not told them they had missed the bus on purpose.

"So we were wandering around trying to find help from one of the rangers," she continued. "Then this man jumped out and started chasing us. He was dressed in a uniform like yours, with a stocking pulled down over his face."

She told them about the chase, and how she had set the trap. Once in a while, Bess and George chimed in. Nancy could tell the rangers were skeptical of their story.

"He went out that way just before you burst in," Nancy said, pointing across the room. "Look—the door is still open."

"Maybe it's open because that's the door you used to break into the palace," the other ranger said, his blue green eyes narrowing as he looked at her.

"We're telling you the truth," Nancy insisted. "Really. If you hurry, you can probably still catch him."

They all walked over to the open door and stepped out onto the patio, which had a short stone wall around it. Nancy knew that beyond the wall were acres of dark canyons full of chaparral and other bushy plants. But the fog was so thick, there was almost no visibility at all.

"If there was such a guy and he went out there, even the dogs would have trouble in this fog," the man said. "You watch these three. I'll see what we can find. If there is someone out there, he may still be hiding nearby."

The woman nodded, and her partner went over to a guard dog leashed to a hook on the side of the patio wall. Silently, they all watched the man and dog leave the area.

Finally, the woman said, "Okay, I'm Ranger Kay Garber. Let me have your names, and I'd like to see some identification, please."

Nancy, George, and Bess gave Ranger Garber their names and addresses and showed her their driver's licenses. The ranger searched their pockets and bags.

Nancy's shoulders stiffened when Ranger Garber pulled out Hubbard's letter. The ranger glanced at the envelope quickly, then handed it back. Nancy's shoulders relaxed. She must think it belongs to me, she thought with a relieved sigh.

She put the yellowed paper back into her pocket. She knew that if she told the rangers where it had come from, they would take it from her. Then I'd probably never get to read it, she thought. I just want to see what he said. Then I'll turn it over to them.

The other ranger, whose name badge identified him as Raymond Horton, returned without the dog. "No sign of anyone here," he said. "The front door of Guest Bungalow B was open. Do you know anything about that?" he asked Nancy and her friends.

"It was open when we peeked in," Nancy said. "We were looking for help."

"Yeah, right," Ranger Horton said. Nancy could tell he still didn't believe them. She slipped her hands into her jacket pockets.

"We'd better take them down to see Sheriff Walsh," Ranger Garber said. "He'll be able to get the truth out of them. Maybe a night or two in jail will help open them up."

Bess clutched Nancy's arm, saying, "Do something. Can't you call your father?"

"I will if I need to," Nancy assured her in a low voice. "Just relax—don't panic."

The rangers drove Nancy, Bess, and George down the mountain to the small town of Seacove. As they drove up the main street to the sheriff's office, they passed Nancy's car parked on the street.

Nancy could tell by Sheriff Walsh's expression that he wasn't happy about being summoned.

"I was watching my favorite television program," he began. "I don't enjoy being hustled away from my program to question three tourists

119

discovered at Cloud Palace after hours. Now, suppose you tell me just what's going on here?"

The rangers explained how they had found Nancy and her friends and about the search that turned up no one else.

"What's your side of the story?" Sheriff Walsh asked, turning to Nancy. She did most of the talking, repeating the story she had given to the rangers.

When George and Bess were questioned, they echoed Nancy's story.

The rangers and Sheriff Walsh still weren't convinced. They questioned Nancy, Bess, and George for over an hour.

The rangers said they thought Nancy and her friends had planned to steal something from the palace. "I'm not saying you were going to walk off with a priceless painting or a rare book," Ranger Horton said. "But I am thinking you might have wanted a few little souvenirs—maybe a teacup or a picture of some celebrity."

"My idea's a little different," Sheriff Walsh said. "You three might have been up there for some other kind of mischief." Nancy heard Bess gasp.

"It wouldn't be the first time a state park has been vandalized," Walsh continued. "Maybe you planned to stuff paper towels down the kitchen sinks or spray paint the marble statues?"

"Absolutely not," Nancy said. "We would never think of doing such things. Please—won't you call Didi Koulakis at the Opa resort in Cliffton?

She'll confirm our identity and vouch for us. You could call Sheriff Jacobs, too," she added. "He knows us."

"Nancy's father is a very prominent attorney," Bess said. "Maybe she should call him and he can set you straight."

Finally, Sheriff Walsh called his fellow lawman in Cliffton and then called Didi. After he hung up from the second call, he turned to Nancy.

"Well, they both think you're okay," he said. "But they admit they've only known you for a few days. So watch your step. We're going to be keeping in close touch with them for a while."

The rangers drove Nancy, Bess, and George back to the parked Mustang. As Nancy pulled away from the curb, she could see in the rearview mirror that they watched as Nancy drove the car all the way up the coast road and out of town.

When she was certain they weren't being followed, Nancy pulled the car off the road. She parked in a small lot set off for tourists who wanted to enjoy a scenic view of the ocean.

"Whoa," George said with a huge sigh. "That was really close. I wasn't sure we were going to get out of that one."

"I'm not sure we are out," Nancy warned.

"You mean what Sheriff Walsh said about watching our step?" Bess asked.

"Not really," Nancy answered. "I'm more worried about the man who threatened us at the palace. Who was he?"

"Maybe *he* was a thief," George said. "And he was planning a robbery—jewels or art or something. We were in his way, so he tried to get rid of us."

"He must have been shocked to find us there," Bess pointed out. "I wonder what he was stealing."

"What if it was Hubbard's letter?" Nancy said.

"But how would he know about it?" George asked.

"We found out about the secret compartment by going through the rubble of the cottage at Opa," Nancy said. "Maybe he did, too."

"But, Nancy," Bess said. "Sam and Barney Shaw wrecked that cottage, and they're in jail."

"Yeah, but what if they have a partner?" George said quickly. "And they told him about it and he came on his own—"

"Or followed us," Bess said, interrupting her cousin. "Oh, now I *am* scared."

"Don't worry," Nancy said. "We'll keep an eye out for him. He should be limping for a few days. If he shows up, that will help us spot him. By the way, did you notice anything familiar about that guy?" Nancy asked.

"What do you mean?" George said.

"I don't know," Nancy said. "Something about the way he moved. I can't figure it out."

She reached inside her pocket for the enve-

122

lope. She pulled out Hubbard's letter and carefully unfolded it. From the backseat, George
flipped the switch for the overhead light.

"This is it," Nancy said, scanning it quickly.
She trembled with excitement. "This letter has
the answer we've been searching for!"

14

A Deceiver Unmasked

"What is it?" Bess asked, as Nancy finished scanning the letter. "Tell us, Nancy."

"It's a letter from Hubbard to a lady friend, Joan Lynn," Nancy told them. "It says he's afraid he's going to die soon. He wants her to have a large stash of gold that he mined. And he gives detailed instructions about how to find it—in a prehistoric cave in Pico Cielo!"

"Oh, wow!" Bess murmured breathlessly. "The legend is true."

"We'd better get back to Opa and get some sleep," Nancy said, starting the car. "We've got a big day tomorrow."

An hour later Nancy parked the car in their space at Opa. The three hurried down the path to their cottage. After a quick snack, they tumbled into their beds. Nancy tucked the letter from Hubbard under her pillow for safekeeping.

When they woke the next morning, they ate doughnuts and juice in the cottage. Still in their sleepshirts, they sat around the breakfast table and read Hubbard's letter again. Nancy got out the map and they planned their trip to Pico Cielo.

While they talked, there was a knock at the door. Bess answered it and welcomed Didi into the cottage.

"You guys got into quite a jam last night," Didi said. "Glad to see you made it home safe."

"We nearly spent the night in the Seacove jail," George said. "Thanks for vouching for us."

"Happy to do it," Didi said with a warm smile. "I know you weren't there to rob the place." She helped herself to a doughnut, then added, "By the way, why *were* you there?"

Nancy filled Didi in on their adventure at the palace and showed her Hubbard's letter.

"This is so exciting," Didi said. "When are you going to the cave? I want to go with you, but I can't get away until after noon."

"I guess we can wait," Nancy said reluctantly. She was eager to get to Pico Cielo and see the mysterious underground world of Hubbard's legend, but she wanted Didi to be part of the adventure, too.

"By the way, did Cal tell you what happened

125

down by the stable Saturday night?" Nancy asked Didi.

"No," Didi said. "What do you mean?"

Nancy told her about the argument Cal had with the stocky man with the red beard. She also told her how the stranger had threatened her until Cal stepped in.

"I hired everyone who worked on the festival. I don't remember hiring anyone who looked like that," Didi said. "Did Cal say where the guy was working during the festival?"

"No, he didn't," Nancy replied.

"That's odd," Didi said. "I'll have to talk to Cal about it."

After Didi left, George grabbed the bathroom first. Nancy and Bess cleared the table and straightened the kitchen while George showered.

"You know, I wonder about Cal," Nancy said. "If the stranger with the red beard wasn't hired for the festival, Cal lied to me. Who was that guy? And why were they arguing? Maybe we ought to do a little checking into Cal's background while we're waiting for Didi."

George came out dressed in jeans, a T-shirt, and her hiking boots. She tied a flannel shirt around her waist.

Bess took her shower next while Nancy sat at the table with her notebook and a pen. "Didi told me Cal came from Montana," Nancy said. "She also said that his hobbies were botany, archaeology, and paleontology. I think I'll try to get some background on him."

"There are paleontological digs in Montana," George pointed out. "Dinosaur skeletons have been found there."

"That should help me track down his history," Nancy said. She called the town library and got the telephone number for the Montana State Board of Health, which would have Cal's birth record. Then she got the numbers for the Bureau of Motor Vehicles, the Superintendent of Public Schools, and several universities and colleges specializing in the field of natural sciences.

Then she started down the list. "Sure wish I had my laptop," she muttered while she waited, on hold, for some information.

After forty-five minutes of dialing, talking, and jotting notes, she finally hung up. Bess emerged from the bedroom dressed in jeans and a sweatshirt.

"Nancy's been checking on Cal," George told her cousin.

Bess took a seat next to Nancy at the table. "What did you find out?" she asked.

"Not much," Nancy said. "It seems that no one by the name of Cal or Calvin Burns was born in Montana, or even went to high school or college there. No Cal Burns ever registered to vote or got a driver's license."

"So what does that mean—that he's not Cal Burns or that he lied about where he's from?" George asked.

"I know he told Didi he came from Montana," Nancy said. "Well, he could be from there without being born there."

"True," George said, "and he could have attended a private high school and not gone to college."

"Or gone someplace out of state," Bess pointed out.

"Right," Nancy said with a nod. "But he probably would have gotten a driver's license somewhere along the way."

"Wait a minute," George said. "Let's say he lied to Didi about where he came from. That doesn't make him a criminal. Maybe he had a personal reason for not saying."

"Okay, but how about this?" Nancy said. "He's supposed to be into paleontology and archaeology, right?"

"Right," George agreed. "And I believe it. He practically gave us a classroom lecture when we went out to the canyon," George added.

"There are several associations and clubs in Montana for people who are interested in the natural sciences. He's never been a member of any of them."

"So what if he lied about his name," Bess said. "What's the big deal?"

"Sometimes it's no big deal at all," Nancy said. "But we've still got unsolved problems here. And he's a man living on the premises who's lied at least once to his employer."

"But what's his motive?" Bess insisted. "He

surely doesn't want to sabotage Opa. If he succeeds, he's out of a job. Of course, if he finds the cave and Hubbard's money, he doesn't need a job."

"Maybe he's not after the money," Nancy said. "Maybe he's interested in the cave itself. Remember the legend. Hubbard said the cave was full of animals and insects that have never seen the light of day. Some of them may be prehistoric. It might be the discovery of the decade."

"Ooh, Nancy, you might be onto something," Bess said, her eyes widening. "Do you think those creatures that Hubbard saw are still in there?"

"Who knows how long they were there before Hubbard saw them?" Nancy asked. "If they were thriving then, they could be now."

"I'm not sure we want to find this cave after all," Bess said with a shudder.

"Are you kidding?" George said. "This may be our most exciting adventure yet!"

"We've still got some time before Didi is going to be free," Nancy said. "Give me a few minutes to get dressed and let's go to the library in Cliffton. There are a few other sources we can check out."

While Bess and George finished tidying up the cottage, Nancy showered and dressed in jeans and a sweater.

When she returned to the living room, she went into the kitchen. In a bottom drawer, she found a screwdriver, a hammer, and a large flashlight. She stuck those, a knife, and Hubbard's instructions to the cave in her backpack. Then she grabbed her jacket and hiking boots.

As she and her friends left the cottage, Nancy grabbed the camping lantern supplied for resort guests who might want to walk the canyons at night. The three then climbed in the car and drove to Cliffton.

The library was small, but it had a computer available to access the network of libraries around the state.

George and Bess checked out current natural science journals and textbooks for articles or chapters by Cal Burns. Nancy used the computer to research older records.

At last she hit the jackpot. As she scanned a ten-year-old science journal, she saw Cal's face. He was identified as prominent paleoecologist Caldwell Burnett.

A quick check of the newspaper files turned up several articles. Dr. Burnett had had a worldwide reputation among scientists for his work on the ecology of prehistoric creatures—how they lived together and interacted.

Nancy called Bess and George over to share the news. " 'Eight years ago,' " Nancy read aloud, " 'Dr. Burnett's reputation was ruined by scandal. He claimed to have found a skull belonging to a prehistoric man. It was later discovered to be a fake. His career destroyed, Dr. Burnett went into hiding, and his whereabouts are unknown.' "

"Well, *we* know where he is," Bess declared.

Nancy printed a few pages of information, then closed out the computer. From a phone booth outside the library, she called Didi and told her what they had discovered. Didi was stunned by the news.

"Don't say anything to him yet," Nancy said. "We have no proof that he's caused any problems."

"But we do have proof of his lying and false identity," Didi said.

"Yes, we do," Nancy agreed. "George, Bess, and I want to go on to the cave since we're nearly halfway there now. Why don't you meet us there when you're free."

"Great," Didi said. "Maybe this fantasy world that Hubbard talked about will cheer me up."

Nancy repeated Hubbard's instructions about where the cave was located. "Remember," Nancy cautioned. "Don't tip off Cal that we know anything about his background. If he's responsible for any of the problems at Opa, he'll disappear if he thinks we're onto him."

"Okay," Didi agreed. "See you soon. 'Bye."

Nancy, George, and Bess drove to the foot of Pico Cielo. Nancy put on her hiking boots and tied her jacket around her waist. Then she grabbed a compass from the glove compartment, and they all walked toward the foot of the mountain.

"Remember," Nancy said, "Hubbard's instructions were written decades ago. The small pine tree that he planted will be a big tree now—or maybe even gone. Keep an eye out for the large pointed boulder and the initials he carved in it with his pickax."

The three fanned out and began searching for the large boulder at the foot of the pine tree that Hubbard had described. They pulled and pushed tree branches and vines away from boulders. After a half hour, they still hadn't found anything matching his description.

Bess slumped down on a small rock and rubbed her arms. Nancy and George joined her.

"Maybe the letter is a hoax," George said, discouraged and grumpy.

Nancy pulled Hubbard's letter out of her backpack and rechecked the compass settings he had listed. "We've done everything right," she said. "But we still can't find— Wait a minute, they've had several earthquakes around here since this letter was written."

"Prehistoric bugs, earthquakes," Bess muttered. "Are you sure we're on vacation?"

"Because of the earthquakes, these compass settings may be off," Nancy pointed out. "The earth has moved a little to the north or south. George, you go farther around the mountain that way. I'll go back this way."

"I'm coming, too," Bess said, scrambling after George.

Nancy watched her friends walk farther north, then she began searching again. Nancy pulled at vines and bushy undergrowth. At last she found it—Hubbard's boulder. She felt like a miner during the gold rush. "I've got it!" she called out.

George and Bess raced to join Nancy. A huge pine tree was anchored solidly at the foot of the mountain. At its base was a large white boulder partially covered with a pale gray-green mossy lichen.

The three used branches to scrape away the plant. At last Nancy stopped. "There they are— the initials we're looking for," she said in a soft voice. "H.W."

"Hubbard Wilson," Bess said breathlessly.

"Come on," Nancy said. "Let's roll this boulder away. The letter says the cave entrance is behind it."

They heaved their weight against the boulder. It rocked back and forth a couple of times. Then with one final lurch, it rolled away, leaving a tangled web of chaparral, roots, and loose dirt.

"The cave should be right here," Nancy said, taking a tentative step forward and pushing at the viney growth.

"I can't wait to see what's in there," George said, pushing forward with a big step.

"George, wait a minute," Nancy said, grabbing for her friend's arm. She was too late. She watched in horror as the loose dirt beneath her friend gave way.

George stumbled and slammed into the roots and bushes, then plunged through the opening into the damp darkness inside the mountain.

15

Earthquake in Wonderland

Nancy and Bess watched George fall with dizzying speed until she disappeared. Then they heard her land with a loud thunk.

"George," Nancy called from above. "George, are you all right?"

"I think so," George called from below. Her words echoed faintly. "I landed on my back. I don't think I'm hurt—just sore."

"Don't move," Nancy said. "We'll be right there." She gave the flashlight to Bess, who beamed it into the gap that had been covered by the boulder. Then Nancy turned on the camping lantern and aimed its light down also.

The cave's limestone walls dripped with moisture. Several yards below, she could see George sitting on a ledge that jutted out from the wall.

Guided by the strong lantern and flashlight

beams, she and Bess moved cautiously through the opening in the tangled roots that George had created with her falling body. There were rough steps hacked out of ledges leading down to the floor of the cave.

"I'll bet Hubbard made these steps with his pickax," Bess murmured.

"Probably so," Nancy said in a low voice.

It was spooky in the cave. The farther they went down, the damper and creepier it was. There was no sound except their own breathing and the far-off *plop-plop* of dripping water.

At last they reached the ledge where George sat, rubbing her shoulder. The three hugged each other in relief. Then Bess helped George pull on the flannel shirt over her bruised shoulder, while Nancy flashed the lantern around the cavern.

Nancy aimed the light beam ahead and located the rest of the handmade steps leading down to the floor of the cave.

"Wait a minute before we start," George said. "I don't know whether my eyes are deceiving me. Turn off your lights and look over there." She pointed toward one side.

Nancy turned off the lantern and Bess flicked off the flashlight. They all gazed where George had pointed.

At first Nancy saw nothing. Then, after her eyes had adjusted to the darkness, she thought she saw a very faint glow in the distance.

"I think I see a dim light," Bess said. "Is that what you mean?"

"Yes," George said. "I saw it while I was waiting for you two to get down here. It changes, too. It gets a little brighter, then fades. Is it a mirage, Nancy? Is it just some trick that the darkness plays on our eyes?"

"I don't think so," Nancy said. "I see it, too. Let's find out. George, are you really all right? Can you walk okay? If you think you need to see a doctor, tell me."

"No, really, I'm fine," George said, standing up awkwardly. "It's just a pulled muscle, I think."

"Okay, let's go," Nancy said, turning the lantern back on. She started stepping down the rest of the ledges to the floor. George and Bess were right behind with the flashlight.

When they reached the bottom, Nancy swung the light around. There were several openings to other rooms. They were in a maze of huge caverns leading back through the mountain. Keeping the lantern aimed at the floor ahead of them, she walked toward the glowing area.

They turned a corner and stepped into a dreamworld. A huge room sparkled with strange neon colors and lights. Shimmering pools were alive with pale, almost transparent fish. Their eye sockets were covered over and useless. Dancing in the lantern and flashlight beams were exotic-looking luminous insects. Some glowed iridescent blue and green. Others shone bright gold.

All of them seemed to have colored lights within their bodies.

Nancy placed the flashlight on one ledge and the lantern on another. Their beams shone out into the room and joined with the lights and sparkles of the creatures. The cavern was filled with a soft golden white glow.

Nancy and her friends wandered around stalagmites and under stalactites. For a few moments, they were so entranced that they couldn't speak.

"Wow," George finally said. "This is unbelievable."

"It's like magic," Bess said. "Like an illusion. I can't believe it's real."

"Hubbard was right," Nancy said. "It's incredible."

As they spoke, the sound of their voices was magnified ten times in the huge room. Echoes resounded in the other rooms leading from this one.

"Whew, it's cold down here," Bess said, pulling on her sweatshirt. Nancy followed suit with her jacket. The lights and shadows and colors in the cavern changed constantly. As the insects darted about and fish jumped and splashed, new shots of color and light shot across the room.

Nancy, Bess, and George jumped when they heard Didi's voice from around the corner. "Nancy?" she called out. She sounded timid and uncertain.

"We're in here," Nancy said, her voice bouncing around the limestone walls. "Just follow the light."

"I . . . I'm not alone," Didi said as she rounded the corner into their room.

Bess gasped as Didi entered, carrying another Opa lantern. She was followed by Cal, who was armed with a pickax and a rifle.

Cal gave Didi a push and she stumbled over to join Nancy, George, and Bess. Cal's mouth dropped open, and he seemed almost hypnotized as he looked around in awe.

"Hello, Dr. Burnett," Nancy said coolly.

His head whipped around, and his eyebrows arched high, revealing his surprise. "So you found out my name," he said. "You are good."

"You've done it," Nancy said, with a broad gesture of her arm. "You're in Hubbard Wilson's prehistoric cave. You can reclaim your reputation as a leader in your field."

Cal smiled as he gazed around. "And the million dollars in sponsorships and grants that will follow, I'm sure," he said.

"Why didn't you tell me who you were?" Didi asked him. Nancy could see she was very upset.

"I'm not sharing this with anyone," Cal said, his eyes narrowing to slits. "I've learned not to trust people."

"Well, we found it first, anyway," Bess said. "So it won't be worth anything to you, after all."

"Did you know about the cave before you came to work for me?" Didi asked.

"Of course," Cal said. "It's the only reason

why I took the job. Why on earth would I do menial work at a failing resort?"

Cradling the rifle in one hand and dangling the pickax from the other, Cal sauntered around the cavern as he talked. He seemed mesmerized by what he saw.

"I had heard about the Hubbard Wilson legend for years, of course," he said. "When the scandal broke, I went into seclusion and formed my plan. When I found out that Pico Cielo might be near or even on Opa, I came and offered you my services."

"Were you behind the original sabotage?" Nancy asked.

"Of course," Cal replied. "I intended to force you out of business, buy the property from bankruptcy court, and then conduct my search in privacy. If the cave was really on Opa, it would be ideal. I would actually own the find. If not, owning Opa would still allow me to search without interference."

He stopped wandering and glared at Nancy. "When Didi asked for your help, I wasn't worried at first. Then I realized you were more capable than I'd thought. You and your friends were beginning to pry in dangerous territory."

"You were there when I talked about the hidden compartment in Hubbard's Opa cottage," Nancy said, remembering. "And you also heard me say that Hubbard had worked at Cloud Palace."

"That's right," Cal confirmed. "I could tell

you were determined to crack the case. I decided to discourage you a little."

"You severed the televison cable," George said angrily. "I could have been killed."

"That was not the point," Cal said. "I wanted to scare you all off. I also wanted to create a distraction long enough so that my ally could check your cottage. I needed to know if you had found out anything that I didn't know about."

"I knew someone had gone through our things that night," Nancy said. "Who is your ally? That red-bearded guy who came after me Saturday night down by the stable?"

"Right again, Ms. Drew," Cal said. "He's a greedy fool I hired locally to help me on occasion. He was trying to blackmail me when you interrupted our little meeting."

Nancy shuddered as she remembered that night. She glanced at the others. Didi was red-faced and breathing heavily. She seemed frustrated and embarrassed at having been deceived by Cal. Bess was pale and shaken. Nancy saw anger in George's eyes.

As Nancy watched Cal, he began pacing back and forth and muttering. She felt a small pebble hit the back of her neck. Then she noticed another pebble fall from the ceiling and land at her feet. When a few more trickled down, she quietly grabbed Didi's arm and nodded her head toward the ceiling. Didi looked up, then looked back at Nancy with alarm.

140

A very slight rumble cascaded through the cave. One of the stalagmites seemed to sway.

"What was that?" Bess said, her voice quavering. "The ground seemed to shake a little."

"Don't worry," Cal said, continuing his pacing. "It's a common impression. People who explore caves—spelunkers—always feel as if the floor and walls are moving."

Nancy noticed that he seemed entranced by the neon insects and fish. He didn't seem to realize more pebbles were falling from the cavern roof.

"Tell us about the explosion on Saturday," Nancy said. "The one in the saganaki booth."

"I substituted the explosive," Cal admitted. "I figured if the Greek Festival was ruined, it would probably be the last straw for Didi. Then I could finally buy Opa."

"You bum," Didi said, her eyes blinking away tears. "You're going to pay for that."

"But it didn't stop Nancy Drew and her friends, now, did it?" Cal said. Nancy noticed that he wasn't looking at them at all anymore. He seemed almost to be talking to himself.

"So I followed them to Cloud Palace," he continued. "I took an earlier tour and then followed them discreetly. After all, they might be onto something. Sure enough, they were."

As he talked, the cavern rumbled again. Didi and Nancy gestured to Bess and George to keep quiet and follow them. Slowly, Nancy and Didi inched back toward an archway leading to another cave. Nancy's pulse raced as she remembered what she'd read in the brochure at the cottage on earthquake preparedness. It said that during an earthquake, you should stand in a doorway to ride out the tremor.

"When I realized Nancy and her friends had left this morning, I stayed close to Didi," Cal rambled on, barely noticing the rest of them inching away. "I eavesdropped on her call from Nancy at the library."

Another rumble began. They heard it before they felt it. Cal stumbled and fell to his knees. He gazed into the pool, still cradling the rifle.

Following Didi's lead, Nancy, Bess, and George planted themselves firmly in the arch as the rumbling increased. Nancy could see Cal's lips moving. But she couldn't hear his words over the tremendous, terrifying noise.

It sounded as if the entire earth were being torn apart above them. As they stood in the arched opening, the earthquake ripped through the cavern.

16

Opa!

"Hold on, girls," Didi yelled. "This is a big one." The earthquake lasted thirty-five seconds. It seemed like forever to Nancy and her friends. As they watched, horrified, an enormous stalactite broke from the ceiling and dropped on Cal, hitting him squarely on the back. He collapsed into the prehistoric pool.

When the tremors finally stopped, Nancy rushed to the pool, followed by Didi. They dragged Cal out of the water and tried to revive him, but it was too late.

Nancy grabbed his pickax and a lantern, and Didi grabbed the rifle. The other lantern and the flashlight had been destroyed by the falling rocks.

Nancy led the others out of the glowing room

and back through the first room toward the steps leading up and out of the mountain. As they made their way carefully across the floor strewn with rubble, Nancy noticed a new glint in the lantern's light.

"Look!" she cried. She pointed to the base of a limestone column, still standing a hundred feet high. Three worn, cracked leather bags, stuffed with glimmering rocks, lay on the floor.

"Hubbard's gold," Didi said in a soft voice.

Bess and George hurriedly gathered the bags, and they continued their journey on up to the cave opening. Several of the steps had broken off. They had to reach up and pull themselves over the broken ones to the next step up.

"Uh-oh," Nancy said, as she reached the top step. "We're closed in. The earthquake must have blocked the entrance with more rocks and dirt."

"I'm so glad you thought to get Cal's pickax," Didi said.

"I'll take the first shift," Nancy said.

The others sat on the ledge step while Nancy attacked the debris at the cave opening.

"I would have thought underground would be the worst place to be in an earthquake," George said. "Why didn't the cave just collapse?"

"Actually, underground can be one of the best places to be in an earthquake," Didi said. "Sometimes people in caves don't even feel the tremors."

"The only problem is that what happened up

on the surface sometimes closes the exit from the underground safe place, right?" Nancy said with a groan as she swung Cal's pickax one more time at the blocked cave entrance.

"Here, let me take a shift," Bess said. "I'll do anything to get out of this place." As Bess began hacking at the rubble with surprising force, Nancy joined the others on the ledge.

"Cal must have followed you out here," she said to Didi.

"Yeah," Didi replied with a nod. "He ambushed me just as I was entering the cave."

"I think I'm almost through!" Bess said. "It's really starting to move."

"We're all starting to move," Nancy said, as the ledge they were on trembled.

"It's an aftershock," Didi yelled. "Come on, everybody, let's get out of here. We sure don't want to be on this ledge!"

Nancy and Didi attacked the opening with their hands, making sure they avoided Bess's swinging.

As they felt the aftershock begin, the four leaned against the last boulder blocking their freedom. With a mighty heave, they rolled it away. Quickly, they scrambled into the chaparral and dirt outside the cave entrance.

They lay there until the short aftershock finished. Then they raced to Nancy's and Didi's cars. Nancy paused for a moment when she saw Cal's truck and remembered his body in the prehistoric cavern. A shiver cascaded down her arms as she climbed into the Mustang for the drive back to Opa.

When they arrived at Opa, Didi immediately phoned Sheriff Jacobs to report what had happened to Cal. Then she and Nancy, Bess, and George surveyed the damage. They were relieved to see that it was minimal. A few outbuildings had collapsed, and a fence was torn apart, but the main structures were fine, and none of the people or animals was injured.

That evening Nancy, George, and Bess were invited to a special dinner in the main dining room. Several of Didi's favorite vendors from the Greek Festival were introduced, including the local women who baked pastries and the men from the saganaki booth.

Jay and Ken were also invited, and they finally brought the volunteer firefighter to meet Nancy. Didi's uncle Nick also joined them.

Word of the discovery of Hubbard's cave had rippled through the area, and reporters had already arrived to interview Didi, Nancy, Bess, and George.

Didi met Nancy, Bess, and George at the door. "Uncle Nick is seeing a therapist for his gambling problem," she said. "He's pretty upbeat about it. He finally seems to realize that he needs help. I'm so grateful. Thanks, Nancy, for pushing us into it."

"I'm just glad you two worked things out," Nancy said.

"Me, too," Didi said. "Sheriff Jacobs just called. They found Cal's body in the cave."

"What a waste," George muttered.

"Uncle Nick and I are meeting with county and state officials tomorrow to see who is entitled to the gold," Didi continued. "The cave was in the section of Pico Cielo that is on Opa property, so Uncle Nick thinks I might get at least part of it. Hubbard left it to Joan Lynn in his letter, of course, and we'll try to find her descendants for a share. You three may even get a finder's fee," she added with a grin.

"Oh, and I talked to Marco and he really is innocent," Didi concluded. "He thought I was ready to give up because of everything that had happened around here. That's why he was so sure he'd get Opa. You'll hear more about it in a minute."

Didi led Nancy and her friends to a large table in the dining room. She introduced them to everyone while Mrs. Myers passed around glasses of sparkling cider and specially prepared Greek dips.

"I have some good news to announce," Didi said. "And after the week we've had, we could use it. I'm happy to say that the earthquake damage at Opa was minimal and will be easy to repair."

She was interrupted by the opening of the dining deck door. Marco and Martina Arias strode to the table and took their places.

"Some of you may be surprised to see the

Ariases as invited guests here. He and I spoke by phone this afternoon, and we have agreed to sit down soon to work out a compromise."

"That is right," Mr. Arias said. "We have learned that Ms. Koulakis needs a stable master."

"And Mr. Arias wants access to the ocean," Didi added. "So I have offered him a deal. I will give his guests easement through Opa to the beach."

"And I will offer the use of my horses and service of my stable master to the guests of Opa," Mr. Arias concluded.

"Uncle Nick is drawing up the papers of agreement," Didi added. "Nancy, we couldn't have done any of this without the help of you, Bess, and George. Thank you so much. I would like to propose a toast."

Everyone stood and held his or her glass high. "To Nancy Drew," Didi said. "She has restored *opa* to Opa!"

American SISTERS

Join different sets of sisters
as they embark on the varied,
sometimes dangerous,
always exciting journeys
that crossed America's landscape!

West Along the Wagon Road, 1852

A *Titanic* Journey Across the Sea, 1912

Voyage to a Free Land, 1630

Adventure on the Wilderness Road, 1775

Crossing the Colorado Rockies, 1864

Down the Rio Grande, 1829

Horseback on the Boston Post Road, 1704

Exploring the Chicago World's Fair, 1893

Pacific Odyssey to California, 1905

by Laurie Lawlor

Published by Simon & Schuster

The Fascinating Story of One of the World's Most Celebrated Naturalists

Celebrating 40 years with the wild chimpanzees

MY LIFE with the CHIMPANZEES

by JANE GOODALL

From the time she was girl, Jane Goodall dreamed of a life spent working with animals. Finally, when she was twenty-six years old, she ventured into the forests of Africa to observe chimpanzees in the wild. On her expeditions she braved the dangers of the jungle and survived encounters with leopards and lions in the African bush. And she got to know an amazing group of wild chimpanzees—intelligent animals whose lives bear a surprising resemblance to our own.

Illustrated with photographs

A Byron Preiss Visual Publications, Inc. Book

Published by Simon & Schuster

2403-0

*Step back in time with Warren and Betsy
through the power of the Instant Commuter invention
and relive, in exciting detail, the greatest
natural disasters of all time...*

PEG KEHRET'S

THE VOLCANO DISASTER
Visit the great volcano eruption of Mount St. Helens
in Washington on May 18, 1980. . . .

THE BLIZZARD DISASTER
Try to survive the terrifying blizzard of
November 11, 1940 in Minnesota. . . .
Iowa's Children's Choice Award Master List

THE FLOOD DISASTER
Can they return to the Johnstown Flood
of May 31, 1889 in time to save lives?
Iowa Children's Choice Award Master List
Florida Sunshine State Award Master List

Published by Simon & Schuster

3017-02